Slam Dunk Sabotage

Frank leaned over to Biff, who was sucking in deep breaths and gulping down his power drink. "It's up to you and me, big guy," he said. "If we can just hold on to the lead—"

"Aaaaaghh!" Biff suddenly cried out. He clutched at his stomach, his face white as death. The plastic bottle he held slipped from his fingers, spilling the power drink on the gym floor. Lurching off the bench, Biff managed to stagger a couple of feet, his body crouched over.

"Biff!" Frank yelled, jumping up to help.

But before he could reach his friend, Biff folded in a spasm of pain. His legs went out from under him, and he crashed to the floor with a sickening thud!

The Hardy Boys Mystery Stories

**Available from MINSTREL Books
and ALADDIN Paperbacks**

140

SLAM DUNK SABOTAGE

FRANKLIN W. DIXON

Aladdin Paperbacks
New York London Toronto Sydney Singapore

First Aladdin Paperbacks edition January 2002
First Minstrel edition October 1996

Copyright © 1996 by Simon & Schuster, Inc.
Produced by Mega-Books, Inc.

ALADDIN PAPERBACKS
An imprint of Simon & Schuster
Children's Publishing Division
1230 Avenue of the Americas
New York, NY 10020

Printed in the U.S.A.

10 9 8 7 6

ISBN 0-671-50526-2

Contents

1 Offensive Foul

"*Bomb*-ers! *Bomb*-ers!" The crowd's chant echoed off the brick walls of the Bayport High gym and rang in Joe Hardy's ears. His brother, Frank, had just passed him the basketball, and now it was Joe's job to keep the Bombers in the running for the conference championship.

As he dribbled in for a layup, Joe's eyes were riveted to the basket, eighteen inches wide, ten feet off the floor. Just as he was pivoting to shoot, he felt an explosion of pain behind his eyes. One second he was racing down the basketball court. The next, he was lying on the hardwood floor, trying to clear the stars that had suddenly appeared in front of his eyes. Joe never saw the elbow that rammed him in the side of the head.

The sound of the referee's whistle slashed through Joe's aching brain. "Rocky River—Number Thirteen," the official said. "Offensive foul."

Glen Revelle, the captain of the opposing team, looked ready to argue. "It wouldn't have happened if Hardy had watched where he was going."

"It was up to you to make sure you didn't clip him," the official replied.

Joe's eyes finally focused again, just in time to see the tall lanky Revelle frown and raise his hand, accepting the foul. Glen's hand went down to rake through his carroty orange hair.

As Joe pushed himself to his feet, the whole gymnasium seemed to throb with noise from cheers and countercheers. At least, that's the way it seemed to his battered head. Bayport Bombers and Rocky River Rockets fans were all stamping their feet so hard that the bleacher seats were vibrating.

Shaking his head to clear it, Joe stepped up to the foul line. Like everyone else in the gym, he knew that this foul shot could win a very tight game.

"Go for it!" Frank urged.

Biff Hooper, the Bombers' big muscular center, flashed Joe a grin. More than a teammate, Biff was a good friend. He gave Joe the thumbs-up sign.

Joe bounced the ball once, twice, three times. Then he stepped away from the foul line. With a trembling hand, Joe pushed his blond hair off a suddenly sweaty forehead. This wasn't a reaction to the blow he'd just taken, he realized. It had just dawned on him that he was about to attempt the biggest foul shot of his basketball career. If Joe made this foul shot, the Bombers would beat the Rockets, and the Bayport team would get to compete in the championship game. If Joe didn't make the shot . . . He sucked in air and pushed that thought away.

Trying to calm himself, Joe swept his eyes quickly around the arena. He saw his girlfriend, Iola Morton, on the sidelines with the rest of the cheerleaders. And Frank's girlfriend, Callie Shaw, was sitting in the stands with Joe's aunt Gertrude and his mother. Joe even spotted Jake Berman, the captain of the second-place Ocean City Slickers. If the Bayport team won today's game, they'd face the Slickers for the championship.

Well, Jake isn't here to cheer me on, Joe thought. He's just scouting us for *his* team's game, to see what he's up against.

Silence fell as what seemed like thousands of eyes stared at him. Joe suddenly felt lightheaded. His palms were so sweaty he could barely hold on to the ball.

Glen Revelle, standing to Joe's right, smirked and said, "Don't choke, Hardy." The Rockets' captain's smile wasn't friendly. It was more like a wolf baring its fangs—except wolves didn't wear braces that gleamed under the gym's bright lights.

"Who asked you, Revelle?" Joe snapped back. The rival captain's taunting was just what Joe needed to regain his focus. No way was he going to let this clown psych him out after knocking him flat.

Joe stepped up to the foul line. He knew what he had to do, and he knew he could do it. One flick of his wrists, and the ball went arcing toward the basket.

Swoosh. The ball sailed through the net.

The hometown side of the gym erupted with cheers. People came spilling out of the bleachers and onto the court, shouting, "We're number one! We're number one!" Excited fans made paper planes out of their game programs. Soon the air in the old high-ceilinged gym was filled with soaring, bright green paper aircraft on victory flybys.

The Bayport Bombers had won! Now they'd play the Ocean City Slickers in two days for the conference championship.

The fans weren't the only ones celebrating the victory. "Way to go, bro!" Frank yelled, wrapping a sweaty arm around Joe's shoulders. At six-foot-one, dark-haired, dark-eyed Frank was the slightly taller brother. But Joe was the more muscular of the two. "One more game! Just one more!" Frank exclaimed.

"We're going all the way," Joe called back as the crowd surged around them. Surrounded by cheering kids and even adults, Joe decided just to let himself enjoy the applause and the pats on the back. Tony Prito, who was also on the team, came up to him for a handshake, followed by Coach Moran.

Iola Morton pushed through the ring of fans and gave Joe a kiss. "Ugh," she said, pulling back. "You're soaking wet."

"Funny how that happens after just an hour of full-court basketball," Joe replied with a grin. "I thought you'd be happy that I went all-out."

"You sure did that," Iola told him. "Now there's nothing standing in the way of us becoming the champs."

"Well, there is that little formality of beating the Ocean City Slickers," Joe reminded her.

"Come on," Iola insisted. "You guys will be playing the final game here in Bayport, with the home-court advantage. And you already beat the Slickers in Ocean City earlier this season."

"Hey, that wasn't an easy win," Joe cautioned. "We barely pulled it off by one point. And that time, the Slickers didn't have their big star on the court. Jake Berman had to sit out the game with an injury. But he looked pretty healthy just now. I saw him in the stands, checking us out."

"That reminds me," Iola said. "Callie came down from the stands with a message. Your mom and aunt wanted to congratulate you, but this mob

5

scene scared them off. Callie said your mother left with Mrs. Jorgensen."

"Right," Joe said. "She'll be out of town for a few days. Mom planned to leave right after the game."

"She also said your aunt took off to go bowling." Iola looked uncertain as she asked, "Was Callie pulling my leg?"

Joe laughed out loud. "Believe it or not, that's how Aunt Gertrude likes to relax." He brushed at the front of his sweat-dampened jersey. "Let me get out of this. And while I'm in the locker room, I'll pass along the message to Frank if Callie didn't find him in this madhouse."

As he turned to go, Joe noticed a commotion in the crowd. Somebody in a Rockets uniform was pushing his way toward the locker room. Even seeing him from the rear, Joe recognized the bright orange hair of Glen Revelle.

"Hey, Glen," Joe called as he caught up with the other boy.

Revelle paid no attention.

Figuring he hadn't been heard over the noise of the crowd, Joe tried to catch Glen by the elbow. "I just wanted to say that you guys played a really great—"

Glen Revelle spun around and angrily shook Joe's hand from his arm. "Bug off, Hardy," he said through clenched teeth. His voice was as steely as the metal braces he wore.

6

Blinking in astonishment, Joe noticed Glen had a weird, glassy-eyed expression. What's this guy's problem? Joe wondered.

"Get out of my way," Revelle threatened. "Before I kill you!"

2 Sore Loser

Frank Hardy caught up with his brother just in time to hear Glen Revelle's wild threat. The tall Rocky River captain abruptly whipped around and shoved his way through the mass of fans.

But he hadn't turned quickly enough to hide something from Frank. Glen was blinking away tears as he headed down the corridor that led to the visiting team's locker rooms.

He must be hurting big-time, Frank thought. Of course, Revelle was a senior. He wouldn't get another chance to lead his team to a championship.

"Nice game, guys." Frank heard a familiar voice behind him. He turned to see Jamal Hawkins with his hand held out, palm up. Joe slapped Jamal's hand, and so did Frank. Although Jamal played for the Rockets, he was a good friend of the Hardys. Frank and Joe played pickup games with Jamal whenever they could.

"Hey, Jamal. What's the deal with Revelle?" Frank asked. "I thought he was just about to deck Joe."

"He probably thought Joe was going to rub it in about us losing," Jamal said. "Glen takes getting beat real personal."

"He should lighten up a little," Frank said. "It's only a game."

"Not to Glen it isn't," Jamal said. "His dad is putting a ton of pressure on him to win a basketball scholarship. I wonder how Glen can even enjoy playing anymore. I know for a fact that he *hates* losing."

At that moment, Joe gave a yell of surprise as he was grabbed from behind in a bear hug and lifted up into the air.

"Hey, Chet. I think you'd better let go of Joe," Frank said. "He's starting to turn blue."

Chet Morton finally released Joe, setting him back down on the basketball court. "I just wanted to congratulate your little brother for getting us into the conference championship game." Chet pounded Joe on the back. "Besides, Joe looks good in blue. It matches his eyes."

"Try congratulating him without crushing his lungs," Frank said. "He'll need them for the next game."

"Not to mention my back," Joe said, wincing in pain as he straightened up. "What would Coach say if he knew you were endangering his players?" Chet was Coach Moran's assistant.

"Hey, I'm just toughening up the team," Chet said. "And as Coach's assistant, it's my job to see that you all refuel after a big game. Let's all meet at Burger Bonanza for a little post-game celebration—maybe with bacon and cheese?" Chet asked.

"Maybe later," Frank said. "I want to catch the Marvin Coates press conference first."

Marvin Coates had been captain of the first Bombers basketball team to win the conference championship twenty-five years ago. Later he became a basketball All-American at an Ivy League school. He was still a legend at Bayport High, as well as one of the town's wealthiest businessmen.

"Where is Coates speaking?" Chet asked.

"Right here in the gym," Frank said.

"Maybe I'll hang out," Chet replied, his eyes scanning the basketball court. News teams, photographers, and camera crews were just beginning to show up. "Sometimes press conferences have caterers come in with snacks."

Frank grinned. "If that happens, they'll be for the press only."

"I used to be a paper boy," Chet said. "Doesn't that count?"

The Hardys rolled their eyes. "Guess again, Chet," Frank said.

After they had showered and changed, Frank and Joe returned to the gymnasium. A podium had been placed in the middle of the basketball court. To the side of the court, the press snapped photos of Coates as he chatted with some local politicians. Finally, the tycoon made his way to the podium, followed by Bayport High's principal.

Principal Chambers stepped up to the microphones, cleared his throat, and after a few more pops from the photographers' flashbulbs, he began his introduction. "His winning ways started on this very court, not so many years ago. He's a credit to our school, to our town, as a sportsman, a businessman, and—"

"A major-league slimeball," came a voice to Frank's right. He wasn't sure he'd heard right, but then the person added, "And a hypocrite, too."

Frank glanced over and saw a kid about his own age standing a few feet away, glaring at Coates with a look of sheer hate. The boy wore dirty blue jeans over heavy boots and a black T-shirt beneath a red-and-black long-sleeved lumberjack shirt. A hooded sweatshirt was tied around his waist by the sleeves. His thick-lensed, wire-rimmed glasses gave him a slightly intellectual look.

When the principal had finished his introduction, Marvin Coates took the podium to roaring

11

applause. "As many of you know, especially you fine folks who live here in Bayport, next Wednesday will mark the twenty-fifth anniversary of the Bayport Bombers' first conference championship—"

The crowd thundered its approval.

"And I plan to donate a state-of-the-art electronic scoreboard to the school gymnasium if the Bombers win."

The cheers echoing through the packed gym cut off Coates's next words. He held up his hands for silence. "*If* the Bombers win." He gave the crowd a warm smile. "Nothing in life comes for free. . . ."

"Liar. Phony. Fraud."

Frank glanced over at the kid again. His hair was dark and curly, cut short. He looked clean enough, in spite of his sloppy clothes. Obviously, this guy had a beef against Marvin Coates. But for all of his insults, the boy wasn't shouting. He was just muttering under his breath.

I guess he was here to see the game, Frank thought. But I've never seen him around the school before.

Nudging Joe, Frank asked in a soft voice, "You know that guy? He looks familiar."

Joe studied the kid for a moment. "That's Todd Coates, Marvin Coates's nephew. We met him once with Phil Cohen. Why?"

"Just curious."

Coates continued his speech, occasionally inter-

12

rupted by cheers from the crowd. But Frank's eyes remained fixed on Todd.

"Why do you suppose Todd's giving his uncle the evil eye?" Frank asked his brother.

Joe shrugged. "Maybe Uncle Marv forgot the birthday check or something."

"He doesn't go to Bayport, does he?" Frank continued.

"Who? Todd? No. He goes to Ocean City High."

"So he had no reason to come to this game, except to rag on his uncle. Don't you find that kind of strange?" Frank pressed.

"Not really. Why?"

"Well, Todd's uncle was a big legend here in this school, but Todd didn't go here." Frank paused. "And he's definitely not here to congratulate his uncle. Do you know anything about his background?"

"No. But Phil might." Joe gave his brother a quizzical look. "What's the big deal about Todd Coates, anyway?"

"Just—"

"Yeah, I know," Joe said, cutting his brother off. "Just *curious.*" Frank's inquisitive nature had gotten the brothers involved in solving many mysteries. The two had inherited this characteristic from their father, Fenton Hardy, a retired police officer who continued to investigate crime.

Joe spotted his father shaking hands with Marvin

13

Coates, who'd stepped away from the podium. The Hardys slipped through the crowd till they reached them.

"Boys!" Fenton exclaimed as Frank and Joe approached him. "Did you ever meet my old teammate Marvin Coates?"

"Glad to meet you, sir," the brothers said in unison. They shook the tycoon's hand.

"You two played some top-notch basketball out there," Mr. Coates said. "Good luck in the championship game. Oh, by the way . . . you boys old enough to vote?"

"Marvin's thinking of going into politics," Fenton explained with a grin.

Coates nodded. "I thought I'd start small. Mayor of Bayport seems about right." Marvin excused himself and walked away from the Hardys, shaking hands as he made his way through the crowd.

"If the election were held right now he'd win by a landslide," Fenton observed. Then he looked around. "Did you see your mother before she left?"

"No. She took off with Mrs. Jorgensen right after the game. She thought you were going to be out of town a lot longer," Joe said.

Frank nodded. "Callie said Mom will be gone all week."

"And Aunt Gertrude went bowling to calm down," Joe said with a chuckle.

"Calm down?" Fenton asked in a slightly worried tone of voice. "From what?"

"We take it you missed the game," Frank said.

"Sorry, boys. I just got here in time for the tail end of Marvin's speech. I meant to get here sooner, but the police needed me to ID some of the suspects in this case I've been working on."

"Tell us about it, Dad," Joe said eagerly.

"Over Chinese food," Fenton promised. "I'll fill you in right after you tell me about this wild game you must have had."

"Great," Joe said. "I'm starving."

"Let's see if Chet wants to join us," Frank added.

Joe blocked Frank's chopsticks with his fork, speared the last jumbo shrimp, and popped it into his mouth.

"Nice interception," Chet said. "Though I wouldn't exactly call it team playing."

"So you must be pretty close to bringing the big cheese down, Dad," Joe said when he finished chewing.

"I wish," Fenton said, dabbing his lips with a napkin. "While you boys hit the boards, the police were putting a full-court press on a major criminal gang based south of here. We nailed a good dozen people today, not to mention confiscating all sorts of equipment. That should shut down their operation. But we still don't have a clue to the mastermind's identity."

"But you expect to catch him, don't you, Dad?" Frank asked.

"I hope so," Fenton replied. "He's bound to slip up eventually. Especially if he's as brazen as the thugs he had working for him. These crooks were placing phony automated teller machines all around the country, in parking lots and shopping malls. They even installed some right outside banks."

"I don't get it," Joe began. "You said the ATMs were spitting back the cards with a message saying the machine was out of order. If the person got his card back, what good did that do the crook?"

"I can guess that much," Frank said. "The machine recorded the account and personal identification number—the PIN. Then the crooks could make phony ATM cards and, using the PIN numbers, start making withdrawals like there was no tomorrow."

"Got it on the first shot, Frank," Fenton said. "They were raking in hundreds of thousands of dollars, perhaps millions, from this scam and at least a dozen others. The FBI is still trying to sort it all out."

"How long has this been going on, Dad?" Frank wanted to know.

"The ATM scam is fairly recent. But we've connected this same team of hoodlums to other crimes. It looks as though they've been in operation for at least the last ten years."

"How did you finally catch onto them?" Joe asked.

"We staked out one of their bogus machines, until a guy with the unlikely name of Nick Vetch came to collect the data. When we caught him, old Nick turned out to have quite a criminal record. Another conviction would have him away for a very long time, so he turned state's evidence. That's how we caught his partner, Henry Desmond, and their boss, Clete Skratos, plus several other people—and their money machines. But we're still chasing after the numero uno of the gang."

Frank dipped an egg roll into a dish of duck sauce. "So, how are you going to nab the kingpin?"

Fenton continued. "If we can figure out what the boss did with the money, how he laundered it, maybe that paper trail will lead us back to him. The case won't be closed until we bust this guy. Otherwise, he could just pick up the pieces and start a new operation."

"I don't understand this laundering business," Chet said. "I know the crooks don't put their money in washing machines. . . ."

The Hardys burst out laughing.

"Not exactly, Chet," Fenton said. "Crooks can't simply walk into a bank with a suitcase full of money and deposit it. Banks have to report cash transactions of ten thousand dollars or more. So the modern crook must find a way to use money so it can't be traced back to him. That's called money laundering. One way of doing this—the way these crooks did it—is to set up phony companies. They use fake invoices that allow the dirty cash to be disguised as proceeds from legitimate sales. Byzantine Importers was the front company for these crooks. Their story was that they dealt in gems and gold, which, of course, never existed."

The waiter brought the check and Fenton pulled his wallet out of his suit-coat pocket. "Speaking of gold . . . I hope I brought my credit card. . . ."

After dinner Fenton dropped his sons and Chet off at the Bayport High parking lot, near Chet's car. Frank and Joe had left their van closer to the school building and said they'd walk across the lot. "If it's okay with you, Dad, we'd like to stop by the rec center for a while," Frank said.

"Going to work on some new plays for the Bombers-Slickers game?" Fenton asked.

Frank gave his father a grin. "Got it on the first shot."

The boys climbed out of the car and, after saying goodbye to Chet, walked through the empty lot. "There's Big Blue," Joe said, pointing to their van, which was parked near the school's main entrance. "At least the guys didn't wrap it in toilet paper as part of their victory celebration."

Frank was reaching into his pocket for the keys when a huge old clunker passed by the van. The car's headlights swung along the wall of the school, spotlighting a human form sitting on the front steps. In the dark, Frank hadn't seen him there. But now he recognized the orange hair sticking out from under the hooded sweatshirt. It was the captain of the losing team.

"What's Glen Revelle still doing here?" he said curiously.

The old car screeched to a halt right in front of the stairs, nearly pinning Glen there. A balding man with rusty gray hair burst from the car.

"Here you are!" the man barked, raising a ham-like fist.

Glen cringed and scrambled up a step to get away from the man.

"How can you call yourself the team captain?" the man bellowed. With his fist still raised in the air, he took a step closer to Glen.

3 Reach Out and Scare Someone

Joe cleared his throat very loudly and walked toward the school steps. "Hi, there," he said to the angered man. "Can we help you?"

The beefy balding man obviously hadn't even noticed the Hardys. He spun around when Joe spoke up. "Name's Revelle," he said when he recovered. "This is my boy." The man jerked a thumb at an unhappy-looking Glen. "I come home from work, and the kid isn't there. So I get to waste my time looking for him while he mopes around here."

The man glared at Glen. "And I know why—I heard it on the radio. You blew it, son!"

"I played hard," Glen said defensively.

"So hard you fouled somebody and let them beat

you," Mr. Revelle said sarcastically. "That's no way to get accepted by a big-time school. Those coaches who were so interested in you—how interested are they gonna be in a team captain who loses his shot at the championship?"

Feeling embarrassed, Joe glanced at his brother, wishing they were anyplace else but here. He knew their presence was only making things worse for Glen.

A pale-faced Glen snapped back, "Gee, thanks for pointing that out, Dad. I guess it's like father, like son. Marvin Coates beat you twenty-five years ago, as you kept reminding me from the time I took my first hook shot. Well, I tried, Dad. I tried really hard. But that didn't stop us from getting beaten. So if I don't get recruited by some hot college, I guess I'm gonna have to live with it. And you'll just have to deal with it, too."

Joe almost expected Mr. Revelle to haul off and belt Glen. Instead, the man began talking as if his son hadn't spoken at all. "You've got to win to impress those college coaches, kid. Especially the ones from the good schools. That's what you need—a good college, a degree in something in case you don't make it to the pros. . . ."

A chill ran down Joe's back as he listened to Mr. Revelle begin what was obviously a favorite lecture. If his father had run on like that, Joe would have quit basketball and taken up knitting. "We'll see you, Glen," he said, giving Frank a let's-get-out-of-here look.

Glen's father seemed to focus on them for the first time. "You boys teammates of Glen's? I don't recognize you from the games I've seen."

"Oh, no, Dad," Glen said, speaking in the same mocking tone he'd used earlier when he taunted Joe on the court. "These are *winners* you're talking to. In fact, that's Joe Hardy, the guy I fouled."

"Winners . . ." Mr. Revelle repeated. "That's what you've got to be if you want to hit the big time like Marvin Coates."

Joe blinked in disbelief. It was as if Mr. Revelle had picked up only one word from his son's response. The older man opened his car door. "Come on, we gotta get home. Too bad you can't be more like this guy here."

For a second, Glen was silent. Then he walked past his father and the open car door. Pulling his hood over his head, he said, "You go home, Dad. Tell Mom I'm okay. I'll grab a burger or something."

Glen had already broken into a run by the time he reached the Hardys' van in the parking lot. But he stopped for one moment before dashing off. He never said a word. He just glared at Joe with red-rimmed, burning eyes. Then he was gone.

"Kids," Mr. Revelle muttered as he got into his car. In a cloud of fumes, the old heap backed up.

Frank opened up the van and got behind the

wheel. "Did you see the way Glen was glaring at you?" he said to Joe, who climbed into the passenger seat. "If looks could kill—"

"I wish his dad hadn't said what he did." Joe made a sour face. "If Glen had a beef with me before, he must *really* hate me now." He glanced at his watch. "You mind if we bag the idea of going to the rec center? It's getting kind of late, and all of a sudden, I'm not up for a lot of practice."

"I know what you mean," Frank said as he turned the van toward home.

The boys had barely walked through the front door when the phone began ringing. Joe snatched up the receiver and announced, "Hardy residence."

A husky voice crackled across the line. "Listen up, Hardy. Lose that Ocean City game or you'll be hurting!"

Then the line went dead.

Joe immediately punched in the numbers for the call-back phone feature, listening intently as the phone rang several times.

Frank entered the kitchen and asked, "Who was it?"

Joe began to answer his brother, but then a voice came on the line. It sounded like an elderly woman.

"Yes . . . um . . . to whom am I speaking?" Joe asked politely.

"Who are you?" the voice returned curtly.

"My name is Joe Hardy."

23

"Why are you calling a pay phone?" the woman asked, her voice softening a little.

"Well, actually, someone just called me from that phone, then hung up. And I wondered if you could tell me if you saw who it was."

"There's no one here now," the woman said.

"Did you see anyone walk away?"

"I do see someone walking into the rec center. A tall boy, wearing a hood. I can't see his face. Of course, my eyes aren't what they used to be—"

"The Bayport rec center?" Joe broke in.

"Yes. Now, if you don't mind—"

"Thank you, ma'am. Have a nice evening," Joe said as he hung up the phone.

"What was that all about?" Frank asked.

"C'mon," Joe said, dashing for the door. "I'll tell you on the way over to the rec center."

By the time Frank got outside, Joe already had the van running. As Frank slid into the passenger seat, Joe gunned the engine, then backed the van down the driveway.

"I thought you didn't want to practice tonight," Frank said.

"Some wiseguy just made a threatening phone call to us. I used the call-back feature, and a woman picked up—at a pay phone by the rec center. She said my caller was a tall type wearing a hood. I thought we'd go and check it out." Joe gave the van more gas.

Frank frowned. "Glen Revelle was wearing a hooded sweatshirt. I wonder if he's our guy."

Joe shrugged. "I was thinking that myself. There's only one way to find out."

The night air had turned cold, and by the time they arrived at the rec center, on the outskirts of town, a thick mist was rolling off the bay. The boys parked the van and hurried to the pay phone near the corner. A frigid ocean breeze numbed their faces as their eyes scanned the surrounding area. Joe saw no one around the rec center. There were only security lights on inside the modern building, and no cars were parked nearby.

"The rec center's closed," Frank observed. He leaned against the side of the van. "It's probably no big deal. Some joker made a nasty phone call—so what? It could have been any one of about a thousand Ocean City Slickers fans. We've been threatened before. It's usually just a lot of hot air."

"You're right, bro. This is probably just a wild-goose chase. You want to call it a night?"

Frank nodded, and the boys headed home for bed.

The next morning Joe came down to breakfast a little late. Frank was reading the newspaper as he finished a bowl of cereal.

As Joe reached for the sports page, Frank spoke in tones of complete disgust. "Well, it looks as if there'll be no outdoor concerts in Bayport this year!"

"What are you talking about?" Joe said.

Frank simply pointed at two front-page items. The first headline read, "Park Bandstand Collapses." The other was in bigger letters: "Bayfront Project Delayed."

Joe frowned, puzzled.

"The park bandstand is where all the summer concerts happen, right?" Frank said. "It blew down last night because the town government hasn't spent any money on upkeep. Why haven't they? Because the plans for this bayfront project called for a big new concert pier. But now investors have been pulling out of the project, so the city winds up with neither."

"Maybe we should vote Marvin Coates in as mayor," Joe said, pouring himself a bowl of cereal and dousing it with milk. "He'd be better than these deadbeats."

Frank flicked the newspaper. "As a matter of fact, Coates is the chairman of the construction committee."

"Gee. How nice that his offices are right there on the harbor," Joe said around a mouthful of cereal. "He can make up the difference with some of those bazillions of bucks he has lying around."

"It doesn't look that way," Frank said, returning the milk carton to the refrigerator. "Marvin Coates announced that he's postponing construction of his new offices until the harbor deal is worked out. It sounds as if he's being cautious.

"I guess that makes sense." Joe scooped up more cereal with his spoon. "The guy's being pretty generous already, offering to donate the money for our new scoreboard. You don't get to be one of the richest men in town by tossing your money around."

"Ready to roll?" Frank asked.

"Ready when you are," Joe said, downing the last of his cereal and grabbing his school books.

After school, the boys had basketball practice. The cheerleaders were on the gymnasium sidelines working on some new cheers for tomorrow's big game. Joe's girlfriend, Iola Morton, was talking to her new friend, Jillie Logan.

Jillie was a pretty girl with long brown hair and dark eyes. She had recently transferred from Ocean City to Bayport High.

Joe watched as Jillie did a series of double cartwheels. She sprang up into the air, shot her legs out high, wide, and perfectly straight before landing lightly on her feet. It was a spectacular spread-eagle.

"Wow! That was great!" Iola said, her gray eyes lighting up with excitement.

"Beautiful," Joe agreed, clapping his hands.

Joe stopped in midclap. His gaze fell upon a sullen-looking boy sitting halfway up the bleachers.

He was wearing a black leather motorcycle jacket. It was Jake Berman, captain of the Ocean City Slickers. Joe glanced over at Frank, who was helping himself to some water from the fifty-gallon cooler. "Hey, Frank. We have company."

Frank looked up into the bleachers, then crushed his paper cup. "He's nuts if he thinks he's going to hang out here and steal our plays. C'mon."

Seconds later, they stood in the seats one row down from Jake Berman, staring at him eye to eye.

"Hello, Hardys," Berman said coolly.

"This is a closed practice, Jake," Frank said.

"Lighten up, guys." Jake fingered the silver medallion that hung at his throat. "What do you think this is, a hidden camera? I'm not here to spy on your lame plays. I want a chance to talk with my girlfriend."

"Jake?"

Joe turned to see Jillie Logan climbing the bleacher stairs. Iola was a few steps behind her. "What are you doing here?" Jillie said in a tense voice. "I told you I don't want to see you anymore."

"I thought we could try again," Jake said in a soft voice.

Jillie shook her head. "I don't think so."

"Let's talk," Jake persisted.

"Let's not." Jillie folded her arms in front of her.

"She doesn't want to see you anymore, Jake," Iola said. She was now standing next to Jillie. "You're history. So, please, just go."

But Jake didn't move.

"Take a hint, Berman," Joe said. "Jillie doesn't want you around, and neither do we."

Berman's face reddened, and he balled his hands into fists.

"Don't start any trouble, Jake," Jillie said in a flat voice.

But Jake was already on his feet.

"What do you think?" Joe said, turning to Frank. "Should we get the coach, or throw him out our—"

He never got to finish his sentence.

Jake's hands rammed into his chest—and Joe toppled backward down the bleacher seats!

4 Dirty Moves

Frank was too late to catch Joe as his brother was flung backward. Taking a flying leap, Frank landed with a crash on the bleacher seats two rows down, where he was able to grab Joe as he tumbled.

Jillie and Iola rushed to the two boys. "Are you all right?" Iola cried.

"I must have died and gone to heaven," Joe said in a dreamy voice, looking up at the girls. "But why are all the angels in cheerleaders' outfits?"

"Joe!" Frank said in concern, leaning over his brother.

Joe gave him a wink, whispering, "Play along with me, bro."

"Will you stop fooling around?" Frank demanded, trying to smother a chuckle. Then he saw someone on the gym floor walking toward them and his laughter died.

The commotion on the bleachers hadn't gone unnoticed. "What's the problem here?" Coach Moran called up to them.

There was a long moment of silence. Then Jillie Logan mumbled, "Jake Berman pushed Joe."

"Come down here, Berman," Coach Moran ordered.

Jake went down the stairs as if each step hurt him. He stood silently before Coach Moran.

"Did you push Joe?"

Berman scowled at Jillie, then turned to the coach. "I couldn't say. Everything happened so fast—"

By this time the basketball team and the cheerleaders had gathered around the coach, who cut Jake off. "Don't act smart with me, kid."

Frank could see the muscles along Jake's jaws bunch as he clamped his mouth shut.

"If you disrupt my practice again," Coach Moran continued, "I guarantee you won't be playing in any championship game."

"Then maybe I should go. Right, Coach?" Jake said. To Frank's ears, the words sounded almost cocky.

Coach Moran shook his head in disgust. "Goodbye, Berman. I let you hold up practice long enough. Perhaps that was your intention."

"All I wanted to do was patch things up with my

31

girlfriend," Jake protested. "Then the Hardys butted in—"

"Berman, button your lips and make tracks. Now!" Coach Moran said sternly.

Berman shrugged and headed away. But after a few strides he turned and pointed a long menacing finger in the Hardys' direction. "I'm going to make you guys pay. All of you. You wait and see."

"Now!" Coach Moran bellowed again.

As Jake Berman skulked off, Coach Moran said to the Hardys, "Guys, do me a favor. For the rest of practice, keep your minds and bodies on the court, okay?"

"Right, Coach," Frank promised.

Joe nodded his agreement as their teammates and the cheerleaders returned to their respective practices.

When they finished, the Hardys showered and headed for the gym exit. They were going to meet Callie and Iola for pizza.

Frank pushed open the gym door and started down the corridor that led to the side exit of the building. Then he stepped back, pinching his nose. The floor was wet and smelled of disinfectant.

"What lamebrain slopped all this stuff around?" Joe demanded. "We could slip and break our necks." His nose wrinkled. "Or end up stinking something awful."

Frank nodded toward the windows in the side exit doors. "There's your answer—Mr. Hooley, the new janitor. I'm afraid he's got a lot to learn about the custodian business."

Outside, Frank could see Mr. Hooley leaning against a handcart filled with cleaning supplies. He was talking to someone, but at first Frank couldn't see who it was. Then the other person passed the windows.

It was Marvin Coates. He took a pen out of his jacket pocket and jotted something down on a piece of paper he'd pulled from the janitor's cart. Coates handed the paper to the janitor, patted him on the arm, and walked away.

"What do you think that was all about?" Joe wondered aloud.

"You got me," Frank said. "Maybe he's trying to win Mr. Hooley's vote for the election." He grinned. "Or maybe those are the measurements for the new scoreboard."

"I like that thought." Joe laughed. "But let's forget about Marvin's note. I think I hear someone calling my name." He patted his stomach, which rumbled hungrily. "And it must be Mr. Pizza telling me my pie is ready."

Frank laughed. "Okay, let's go."

A few minutes later, the Hardys strolled into Mr. Pizza. The sight and smell of pepperoni and melting cheese made Frank's mouth water. They slid into a booth already occupied by Callie, Iola, Jillie, and Chet.

Jillie immediately began to apologize. "Hey guys, I'm sorry—"

Frank held up his hand to silence her. "You don't have to apologize for Jake—"

"But—" Jillie interrupted him.

"If Berman tries anything, we'll have the last laugh. You can trust me on that," Joe added.

"I meant the *pizza*," Jillie finally said. "I'm sorry we didn't save you any."

Chet looked up with an air of innocence as he stuffed the last piece of pizza into his mouth. "Oh, sorry. I didn't know Frank and Joe were coming."

"Yeah, right. Tell me another one," Joe joked.

Frank signaled the waitress and ordered another large pie.

"We were talking about the new scoreboard Marvin Coates is donating," Callie said. "I hear it's going to have a camera mounted on it that can show instant replays on a giant monitor."

"*Four* monitors," Chet said. "This thing will be state of the art, all the way. It'll be like a huge cube, with giant screens on each side. No matter where you're seated, you'll see all the action."

"Including some close-ups of the cheerleaders, I hope," Iola said.

"Hey, that sounds good to me!" Joe cracked. Iola elbowed Joe hard in the ribs and he laughed.

"Today's paper said the scoreboard is supposed to cost a million dollars," Jillie said as Frank scooted over to make room for Phil Cohen, who had just joined them. "That's more than the whole sports budget for my school last year."

"Coates can afford it," Chet said, taking a slice from the new pizza the waitress placed on the table. "The guy's rich with a capital *R*. Made a fortune in the import-export business."

"You know, this scoreboard thing isn't a done deal," Phil reminded everyone. "Everybody is saying that the Slickers are seven-point favorites. And that's in *our* gym. It could be a blowout."

"Who pays attention to point spreads, anyway?" Joe said, grinning.

"My dad told me Marvin Coates has all the money in the world," Iola said.

"So why doesn't he bankroll the bayfront project?" Frank asked, recalling the articles he'd read that morning.

"Maybe his cash is tied up in investments," Callie reasoned. "It's not like these rich guys keep all their money in their mattresses."

"And running for mayor can eat up a chunk of change. Campaigns don't come cheap," Chet added.

"Speaking of Marvin Coates," Frank said, shifting his gaze to Phil, "you know his nephew, don't you?"

"You mean Todd?" Phil shrugged. "I *used* to know him as well as anyone can get to know that guy. We were in the same computer club together at the rec center before he quit. He's a brilliant hacker. Temperamental but brilliant." Phil helped himself to a slice of pizza.

"Why'd he quit?" Frank asked.

"There was a big stink about him releasing a computer virus or something. No one could prove it, but most everyone believed it. It just seemed like something Todd would do. He's kind of a rebel, like the way he'd dump on his uncle, saying all businessmen were crooks. Anyway, after the rumor about the computer virus spread, everybody in the computer club kept giving him funny looks. I think it got to him finally. One day he just stormed out and never came back—"

Phil's words were cut short when Jamal appeared at their table. He looked as if he'd just come off the basketball court. "I was hoping I'd find you guys here."

"What's up?" Frank asked.

"I was playing a little one-on-one at the rec center with Glen Revelle when Jake Berman showed up. Jake was mouthing off about how you and Joe made him look bad in front of his girlfriend."

"*Ex*-girlfriend," Jillie corrected.

"Jake didn't need our help to look bad," Joe added. "He managed to do that all by himself."

"Yeah, well, maybe," Jamal said. "But he seemed pretty bent out of shape. I just wanted you guys to know. Jake has some rough friends. Sometimes they get carried away."

"Maybe they were already at work, making threatening phone calls," Joe added.

Everyone at the table turned to stare at Joe.

"What phone call?" Jamal asked.

"Have a seat, Jamal," Joe said. "This could take a while. And help yourself," he added, nodding to the pizza.

"Thanks." Jamal pulled up a chair. He ordered a large cola and took a slice.

Joe told Jamal and the others at the table about the previous night's phone call.

"So you think it was Jake who made the call?" Iola asked. She gave Jillie a nervous look.

"Not necessarily," Frank objected. "It could have been one of Jake's punk friends, trying to lend a helping hand. Jake might not even know it happened." He shrugged. "Although I don't think he'd mind right now. Not only are we rivals on the court, but he dislikes us up close and personal, too."

Joe frowned. "That lady at the phone booth said she saw someone walking away who was tall and wearing a hood."

"So you think it was a hood in a hood?" Callie joked.

But Joe didn't laugh. "I keep thinking that Glen Revelle was wearing a hooded sweatshirt last night."

37

"He was really upset when he lost the game to us." Frank nodded thoughtfully. "And listening to his father chew him out didn't help."

"So you think Glen made that call?" Jamal asked.

"But why?" a puzzled Phil Cohen wanted to know. "I mean, his team is out. It's a done deal. We're playing the Slickers for the championship."

"Glen's sort of friendly with Jake Berman," Jamal admitted. "They spent some summers together at basketball camps. Maybe they're both up to something together." Jamal shook his head vigorously. "I know Glen, though. He may be an intense guy, but he's not a punk like Jake Berman. If Glen did make the call, he was probably just blowing off steam."

They finished up the last of the pizza and everyone got up to leave.

"Jillie and I are going to the mall," Iola announced. "Anyone else want to come?"

"Count me in," Callie said.

"No, thanks," Joe said. "Frank and I have to go to the rec center and work out. Right, Frank?"

"Uh, right." Frank agreed, realizing what his brother was up to. He knew that shopping wasn't Joe's idea of fun.

The group split up. Phil left with some of his friends who had been sitting at another table. Frank and Joe gave Jamal a lift to the rec center. Jamal was still in his sweats and headed right for the gym. The Hardys went to the locker room.

Frank opened his locker and pulled out his running gear. "I'm going to go for a run. You want to come along?"

"I'm going to pump some iron. Catch me in the weight room in half an hour," Joe said.

"Okay," Frank said, lacing up his running shoes. "Don't strain a brain muscle."

Frank hurried outside and began to jog toward a well-beaten path behind the rec center. He ran up a steep incline and along the rim of the woods. Ominous dark clouds were rolling across the dusky sky.

As Frank continued up the winding path, the wind shrieked, bending the treetops sharply. Definitely a storm on the way, he thought. He decided to head back to the rec center before he got drenched.

But as Frank turned, something seemed to explode out of the woods, ramming into him from behind with the force of a battering ram.

Frank had time for one yell of surprise as he found himself flung down the steep dirt embankment. A tree trunk seemed to appear out of nowhere to knock the wind out of him. When he bounced off that, he rolled some more until he struck his head on a rock jutting out of the dirt.

Finally he hit bottom, landing badly on one leg. For a second his vision disappeared in a flare of white as pain seared its way up from his ankle.

Frank pushed himself up on his hands and knees.

39

Little stars began to swirl madly inside his head. But he strained his eyes, searching upward along the steep hillside. At first, all he could see was the ragged outline of bending treetops, moving black branches against a blacker sky.

Then Frank made out a human figure standing on the hilltop, a shadow in a shadow staring down at him.

Frank leaped to his feet, trying to focus, to catch some detail that might identify his attacker. Above him, something glittered in the moonlight.

But as Frank's weight came down on his injured ankle, a new blast of pain washed over him.

It was too much for his battered body. The gleam disappeared as blackness blotted out Frank's mind.

5 Pumped Up

"C'mon, Joe, one more. Give me one more," Jamal urged.

At the bench press, Joe grunted as he pushed the heavy weights above his chest. His arms trembled from the strain. Just when it felt as if the weights might crash down on him, Jamal snatched the bar. Together they raised the barbell back up onto its stand.

Jamal rolled his eyes. "Ten repetitions at two-twenty-five. That's bench-pressing some pretty serious weight. Too bad you can't pump your brain up just as easily."

Joe chuckled. "You sound like my brother." He glanced at the clock on the weight-room wall.

Frank should have been back by now, and Frank was seldom late.

Suddenly, the wail of sirens ripped through the still of the night. Joe sat bolt upright. As the sirens grew louder, nearer, Joe broke out into a sweat. "Frank," he said in a choked voice.

Joe ran outside, followed by Jamal. A police cruiser with an EMS wagon on its tail shot past them, heading up the hill, toward the jogging path. As the realization hit him, Joe sucked in his breath. Already pumped up from his workout, Joe bolted up the hard dirt trail. Something had happened to Frank!

The voice from the telephone the night before echoed in Joe's mind: "Lose that Ocean City game or you'll be hurting!"

Maybe Frank was hurting now, Joe thought, picking up his pace. He didn't slow down until he reached the top of the incline. His chest heaving, Joe stared down the sharply sloping hillside as the twirling emergency vehicle's lights played across his face. They were bringing someone up in a stretcher, and the sight twisted Joe's stomach into a knot.

It was Frank.

As the ambulance crew reached the hilltop, Joe let out a huge sigh of relief. Frank was sitting up. He couldn't be too seriously injured.

"I'm okay," Frank was saying. "Just twisted my ankle." He spotted Joe and Jamal. They were out of breath from their long run up the hill and were still panting heavily. "What took you guys so long?" Frank asked, grinning crookedly.

"I think your brother's all right," Jamal said breathlessly.

Frank swung his feet out over the stretcher and was about to step down.

"Only a nut would try to walk on that foot," the first paramedic said. "It could be broken."

"If you're smart, you'll let us take you to the hospital," the second paramedic said. "That ankle should be X-rayed."

Frank pointed to Joe and Jamal. "Don't worry about it. I have my friends here to help me." Then he looked curiously at the police officers. "Do you mind if I ask who called you guys?"

"We received a 911 call that someone had pushed you down this hill," the first officer, a sergeant, said. He was tall with just the hint of a potbelly beginning to show.

"Who made the call?" Frank asked.

"He said you had been *pushed*," the second officer said, ignoring Frank's question. She was a dark-haired woman with high cheekbones.

"No kidding?" Frank raised his eyebrows and looked innocent.

The female officer frowned. Studying her face, Joe thought she might be a Native American.

"Were you pushed?" the woman pressed. She pulled a report pad from her belt and opened it.

43

Frank avoided the officer's question. "Who made the call?" he asked again. "Do you know?"

"We don't have that information," the sergeant said, crossing his arms in front of him. "Why do you want to know?"

"Just wanted to thank the good Samaritan."

The sergeant narrowed his eyes. "You're Frank Hardy, aren't you? I've seen you around the station house with your dad a few times."

Frank nodded.

"I'm Sergeant Tim Talcott. This is my partner, Sue Birdsong." His gaze took in Joe. "You two are detectives like your old man, aren't you?"

When the boys nodded, the sergeant gave them a big knowing smile. "And you're into something you shouldn't be, right?"

"Actually, we're not investigating—" Joe began.

But Sergeant Talcott broke in. "Listen, kids, there's a time to quit playing private eye and leave the work to the police," he said. "It's our job, and we've been trained to do it."

"We've solved more than our share of crimes, sir. Serious crimes, committed by pros." Joe was getting a little annoyed at the officer's tone of voice. "There's nothing amateurish about our detective work. We do our job well."

Sergeant Talcott nodded. "Didn't mean to insult you. I'm just trying to do my job. If a crime has been committed, I want to know about it."

Suddenly, the police-cruiser radio barked. Officer Birdsong rushed to answer it, climbing in behind the steering wheel. "Let's go, Tim!" she yelled. "We've got a B-and-E in progress."

Sergeant Talcott dashed to the police cruiser, and Officer Birdsong tore away with the siren blaring. The boys watched as the car sped down the hill and away into the night. When the taillights blinked away to nothing, Frank thanked the paramedics for their help, and they reboarded their ambulance.

"You're lucky they got that breaking-and-entering call. Why the big coverup?" Joe asked his brother as the EMS wagon rumbled past them and down the hill. He had easily seen through Frank's flimsy lies. "Who attacked you?"

"I don't know. But I wanted to check something out right away. And that would have been impossible if we were at the station house filling out police reports."

Frank limped over to the spot in the woods where he had seen something glitter. Joe and Jamal joined him, helping to search the area.

"Look!" Frank said, pointing at the ground. "Boot prints."

Joe and Jamal kneeled down next to Frank and examined the tracks in the soft ground. "I'd say these were left by heavy-duty work boots," Joe said. "Look how clear the tread marks are. That means new boots."

"Or old boots with new soles," Frank said.

"So you think these were left by the person who attacked you?" Jamal asked, examining the prints.

"Look at how they're laid out—as if the person were pacing or moving around in place. To stay warm, maybe, while he waited for me." Frank sat on the cold ground to tie the laces on his sneaker. His pant leg was rolled up, revealing the swollen ankle.

"You'd better ice that ankle, man," Jamal said. "It's starting to swell up."

"Later," Frank said, tying his sneaker loosely.

"You really should take care of it," Joe said, shifting his gaze to Frank's ankle. "We have a big game tomorrow."

"By tomorrow, whatever clues are here may be gone. This wasn't an accident, guys. Someone pushed me. And I intend to find out who!" Frank insisted.

"Why don't you two keep looking around while I get the van," Jamal suggested. "I'll bring it back up here so you don't have to walk all the way down the hill on that ankle, Frank." Jamal shivered. "I wouldn't mind getting warm. Man, it is *cold* out here."

"Thanks, Jamal," Joe said, tossing him the keys. Jamal went for the van as the Hardys continued to search the area.

A brightly colored piece of paper caught Joe's eye. "Hey, look at this." He untangled a crumpled green paper airplane that was caught on the branch of a bush next to the footprints.

Joe unfolded the paper. It was a program from the previous day's game. A phone number was scrawled along one wing.

"How did this get here?" he wondered aloud.

"Whoever was waiting for me tonight must have been at yesterday's game," Frank reasoned.

"Did you get a look at this guy?" Joe asked.

"Not till I hit bottom, and then I was pretty dazed. But I saw something glitter up here, something shiny, metallic."

Joe looked puzzled. "Like what?"

"Maybe it was a silver medallion around someone's neck," Frank mused.

Joe took that in for a second. "Like the one Jake Berman wears?"

Frank nodded.

"And what about Revelle?" Joe wondered aloud.

"Revelle?"

"He's got braces. I saw them shining on the basketball court."

Again Frank nodded. "Right now, we know just one thing for sure. This is more than somebody being a bad sport. Whoever pushed me is *serious* about us losing that game tomorrow."

Joe stared down to the bottom of the deep ravine. "You could have been killed."

Jamal pulled the van next to the Hardys and hopped out.

"Where to?" Joe asked as he got behind the wheel. Jamal and Frank got in, and Joe started down the hill.

"Let's start with Jake Berman," Frank said, turning to tell Jamal about the clue they'd found. "Jake was at the game yesterday. He could have made that threatening phone call, too."

"Sounds good to me," Joe said. "As captain of the Ocean City Slickers, he definitely has a motive for wanting to bench you with an injury. Anybody have an idea where we can find him?"

"You could try his house," Jamal said. "Jake lives in Ocean City, over by the mall."

Joe's eyebrows shot up as he glanced at his friend. "Since when do you hang with Jake Berman?"

"Like I said, Glen and Jake are buds," Jamal explained. "Glen invited me to one of Jake's parties. And let me tell you, if you think Jake is bad, wait till you see the guys *he* hangs with. This could get dangerous."

"I want him to see me," Frank said, "and I want to check out his face when he does. Whoever pushed me down that hill figures I'm in the hospital right now. If Berman acts surprised that I'm up and around—"

"He'll be suspect number one," Joe finished. "So we'll just take a drive by. Where does Berman live?" Joe asked Jamal.

Jamal gave them the address. "Just be careful,

guys," he said as he got out of the van in front of the rec center.

Joe rolled the window down and said, "You sure you don't want a ride home, Jamal?"

Jamal shook his head. "I'm going to go work out a bit more. See you at the game tomorrow."

Joe shifted the van into drive and headed toward Ocean City. Jake Berman's house was exactly where Jamal had said it would be. There were no lights on in the house, which seemed empty.

Joe spun the van around and parked on the opposite side of the street. The boys sat quietly in the van for a few moments, then Joe shut the engine down and turned off the lights.

"What now?" Joe asked.

Before Frank could answer, a souped-up Chevy rumbled down the street and pulled into Berman's driveway.

"There he is," Joe whispered.

Berman got out of his car and walked straight up to the Hardys' van. He rapped heavily on the driver's-side window with his knuckles. Joe rolled the window down.

"Nice van," Berman said in a mocking voice. "Be a shame if something happened to it, just because of the dumb way you parked."

Joe could feel his face growing warm with anger. "I parked just fine."

"Except you picked the wrong street," Berman told him. "What do you think you're doing?"

Frank came around the van and walked toward Berman. Joe could see he was trying hard to hide his limp. "Just a friendly visit, Jake. Where have you been?"

"None of your business."

Joe opened the van door and stepped down to the ground. He noticed the shiny medallion hung around Jake's neck, dangling outside his leather jacket. "What went wrong tonight?" Joe said. "Did some little old lady scare you off, Mr. Tough Guy?"

"Huh? What are you talking about?" Berman gave the Hardys what appeared to be a genuinely puzzled look.

Frank studied Jake's face for a long minute. "Nothing. Good night, Jake." The Hardys climbed back into the van. Joe started it up and got the heater going.

"He didn't seem surprised to see me," Frank said. "He had sneakers on, too. The prints in the dirt on the hill were definitely made by a boot."

"So you don't think Jake is the one who pushed you?" Joe said as he turned on the radio and started toward home.

Frank shook his head. "Not unless he's as good an actor as he is a basketball player."

"So where does that leave us?" Joe asked.

"Let's call the number on the program we found." Frank took out the crumpled piece of paper and punched the number into their car phone.

The boys waited anxiously while it rang and rang. No one answered.

"Oh, well," Joe said with a shrug. "We'll try again later."

Joe parked the van in the driveway, and the boys entered the kitchen through the back door. Frank yanked the kitchen wall phone out of its cradle and punched the preset button for the Bayport police.

"What's up?" Joe asked.

"I want to find out the name of that 911 caller. According to the police, he was at a mall. And right now he's the only witness we know about."

"The police won't reveal the caller's identity. You know that." Joe opened the refrigerator and peered inside. "You in for a little leftover meatloaf?"

"Sounds good."

Joe layered slices of meatloaf and cheese onto bread and popped the sandwiches into the toaster oven.

"If Con Riley has desk duty, we might get the information we need," Frank said hopefully. "He's helped us out before."

Joe shrugged. "I guess it's worth a try."

Frank was leaning against the wall with the receiver pressed to his ear. "Yes, hello?" Frank abruptly said. "Is Con Riley there? This is Frank Hardy. . . . Well, I was hoping he could help me. . . . I need the number of a 911 caller. . . . But

51

it's really important. . . . Are you sure? Hello? Hello?" Frank hung up the phone with a defeated sigh.

"I guess it's just not our lucky day?" Joe asked. As Frank shook his head. "Not—"

The rest of his answer was lost, however—as the kitchen window suddenly exploded!

6 On the Ball

Frank and Joe spent the next couple of seconds ducking as shards of jagged glass flew through the kitchen. Joe then ran through the kitchen doorway, taking shelter in the hallway. Frank just dropped to the floor.

For a long moment, they stayed frozen in silence, waiting for another possible onslaught. Then Frank saw Joe peek into the room.

"What was that?" Joe asked in a whisper. "A bomb?"

"There's only one way to find out," Frank said, cautiously heading for the window. Suddenly, he stopped and began laughing. "I guess you could call it a *long bomb.*" He picked up a basketball out of the sink.

Joe looked at the shattered glass all over the floor. "Looks like about a million-pointer," he said glumly. "Hey, what's that?"

Frank rolled the ball over in his hands. "There's a note here, taped to the ball."

Together, the Hardys read the typed words: *"Tonight was just a warning. Take a hint. Don't play in tomorrow's game."*

"Let's have a look outside," Frank suggested. "Maybe whoever tossed this our way left some clues."

Frank was heading out of the kitchen when he heard footsteps in the hall, coming from the front door. Was the smashed window only a distraction to cover someone breaking into the house?

He quickly snapped off the kitchen lights and joined his brother crouching behind the table. The kitchen door slowly creaked open. Frank could see the figure of a man in a suit peering around.

Taking a deep breath, Frank brought the basketball back, ready to hurl it in the guy's face and rush him.

But a familiar scent tickled Frank's nostrils. "Dad?"

"Frank?"

Fenton Hardy flicked the kitchen lights back on and stared at his sons.

"Lucky thing Aunt Gertrude gave you that stinky aftershave for your birthday, Dad." Frank grinned at his father. "We thought you were a burglar."

"That's what I thought *I* was facing when I pulled up and heard glass breaking," Fenton said.

Frank glanced upward. "I guess we should be glad all this ruckus didn't wake up Aunt Gertrude." He lowered his voice. "Otherwise, we'd have the police on the way, too."

"Gertrude isn't home," Fenton said. "I was just coming back after dropping her off at a sick friend's house." He looked around at the wreckage on the kitchen floor. "Now, would you boys mind telling me what this is all about?"

Frank held out the basketball. "Somebody smashed this through the window."

"And this was attached to it." Joe waved the note.

After shaking some glass off a kitchen chair, Fenton sat down and read the note. Then he looked up at his sons. "It looks as though basketball has become a lot rougher game since the days when I was playing."

Frank peered out the broken window. "Whoever did this probably hopped the back fence."

"Probably," Fenton agreed. "I didn't see anyone making a getaway from the front." He looked at his sons. "Somebody obviously doesn't want you playing in tomorrow's game. You boys want to tell me *why* somebody would go this far?"

While Joe went outside to look for clues to who threw the basketball, Frank told his father about getting pushed down the hill.

55

A few minutes later, Joe walked back in. "I found a set of footprints near the window," he said. "They're a perfect match."

Fenton gave Joe a blank look. "A match to what?" he asked.

The boys finished up the story of finding the boot prints behind the rec center. Fenton leaned back in the kitchen chair, staring at the broken window, deep in thought. "So, you're pretty sure it wasn't the Slickers' captain, Jake Berman."

Frank nodded. "I think he's the type who'd brag about dumping me down the hill. The boot marks were exactly where I saw the reflection of light. But Jake was wearing his basketball sneakers when we saw him outside his house a little while ago."

"This Glen Revelle you mentioned," Fenton said. "It sounds as though he was under a lot of pressure to win that game."

Frank nodded.

"You should have seen him when he lost yesterday," Joe said, "and when his father rubbed it in. Maybe Glen just snapped. He really wanted a basketball scholarship."

Fenton took a deep breath. "You boys had better find something to block that broken window," he said. "I think there are some boards in the garage."

Joe grabbed a broom from the utility closet and began to sweep up the mess.

"Do you think you could find out who made a 911 call, Dad?" Frank asked, explaining about the mystery caller who sent the rescue crew to Frank at the rec center.

"I might be able to pull a few strings down at headquarters." Fenton stood up and yawned. "But right now I just want to get some sleep. This case has been one of my tougher ones."

"What's the status?" Frank asked.

"The fox is still on the loose," Fenton said. "Clete Skratos, and his goons, Desmond and Vetch, aren't talking, or else they don't know who's been pulling the strings." Fenton suddenly frowned and grew stiff.

Joe held the broom like a weapon, while Frank tried to peer into the darkness outside the window. "What is it, Dad?" he whispered.

"Just my detective's instinct," Fenton replied.

"Someone outside?" Frank asked softly.

Fenton shook his head and sniffed. "More like something in the toaster oven . . . and I think it's burning."

Frank was putting his books away in his locker after school when Phil Cohen walked up to him.

"Good luck in today's game, Frank," Phil said, slapping him on the back.

"Thanks, buddy."

"How's the injury?" Phil asked.

"What injury?" Callie Shaw had just joined them, and she looked concerned.

Phil ignored Frank's warning look. "Someone pushed Frank down a hill last night."

"Frank!" Callie exclaimed. "Are you all right?"

"Fine," Frank lied. Actually his throbbing ankle had woken him up at dawn. He'd iced it, but it was still slightly tender.

"Let's hope you don't have to guard Berman," Phil said.

"Joe drew that lucky assignment," Frank said as he slammed his locker shut.

"Wait a minute, wait a minute," Callie said, grabbing Frank's sleeve. "Someone *pushed* you down a hill. You mean, on purpose?"

Frank appreciated Callie's concern, but he had an important game to play in less than an hour. He had to keep his mind focused. "I'll tell you about it later, after the game," Frank promised Callie.

Callie obviously wasn't happy about having to wait for an explanation. She turned to Phil and asked, "Who told you this?"

"Some guy in the cafeteria."

"And what exactly did this guy in the cafeteria say?" Callie pressed.

Frank left Phil to explain everything to Callie. He had purposely tried to tone down any stories about his injury. If Coach Moran knew about his damaged ankle, he might not let him play. And no way am I going to miss this game, Frank promised himself. It was the most important game of his high school career.

"Whoa, there!" a voice interrupted his thoughts. It was Mr. Hooley, the school janitor. Frank had almost crashed into his cart of cleaning supplies.

"You're one of the guys on the basketball team, aren't you?" the custodian asked. "Principal Chambers would fire me for sure if I let *you* get hurt right before the big game."

Where were you when I was getting pushed down that hill last night? Frank thought.

"Thanks, Mr. Hooley," he said aloud. Frank was just heading for the stairs when a strange sound filled the air.

Beep! Beep! Beep!

Frank turned to see where the high-pitched tweeting noise was coming from. He saw Mr. Hooley quickly clapping a hand to the electronic beeper on his belt.

The janitor glanced nervously at Frank. "I guess I better get going. Looks like, uh, the principal is trying to find me." He gave Frank a lopsided smile. "If I'd known just how much work this job was going to be . . ."

Chuckling, Frank continued his way down the stairs. It seemed as if high technology was even finding its way into low-tech labor nowadays.

Frank reached the locker room and changed into his basketball uniform. He was just finishing taping up his swollen ankle when Chet sat down on the bench next to him.

"Whooo! That is really nasty-looking." Chet made a face. "Does the coach know you're hurt?"

Frank knew that as the coach's assistant, it was Chet's job to keep an eye out for the players. But this was one time Frank wished his friend wasn't so observant.

"If Coach Moran knows I'm hurting, he'll keep me out of the game," Frank said seriously. "And then whoever pushed me will get just what he wanted."

"Who'll get what he wanted?" Chet asked, confused.

Frank told Chet about what happened the night before. Phil joined Chet and Frank on the bench just as Frank was saying, "Joe thinks Glen Revelle may have done it."

"I don't know about Glen Revelle doing something like that," Phil said. "He's a sore loser, but that's carrying it a bit too far."

"Unless he did it for his friend Jake," Frank pointed out.

"I can see Berman doing it," Phil admitted. "Todd told me he's the biggest bully at Ocean City High."

Frank glanced sharply at Phil. "Todd Coates?"

Phil nodded. "He says Berman and his bully friends have been picking on him since day one."

"Speaking of Todd, what exactly is his relationship with his uncle, Marvin Coates?" Frank asked Phil.

"Not so hot," Phil answered uncomfortably. "Todd's parents travel a lot for business, so Todd lives with his uncle. He even works for him part-time. I remember Todd telling me he has his own office at his uncle's waterfront building. But it's not one big happy family. Todd and his uncle have never gotten along. At least that's the way Todd tells it."

"Marvin Coates seems okay to me," Chet said.

Phil shrugged. "Todd's a strange guy. I bumped into him last night. He was asking me a bunch of stuff about you and Joe."

Frank raised his eyebrows questioningly. "What exactly did he want to know?"

"Oh, the usual when guys hear stories about you being investigators. Todd wanted to know if you were as good detectives as his uncle was making you out to be."

"Why would he want to know that?" Frank asked. As much as possible, Frank and Joe liked to keep their status as detectives under cover. It was easier to work on a case if no one knew the truth about them. But now Todd knows Frank thought. That's not good news.

"I don't know," Phil said with a shrug. "I haven't spoken to the guy in ages, and the first thing he asks me about is the famous Hardy brothers."

"How did his uncle know we were detectives?" Frank pressed.

"You know how it is. Marvin Coates is a big

enchilada in this town," Phil said. "He knows everything about everybody."

"I have a theory about Todd," Chet said. "You know how everyone's making a big deal about Marvin Coates's donation to Bayport High if the Bombers win and all?"

"I'll say," Phil broke in. "A lot of people think Coates made the offer just for the publicity, because he's thinking of running for mayor. But from what I've seen of him, I think the guy is for real. He cares about Bayport. He wants to develop the bayfront so local people can get more jobs. He's a hard worker, judging from the bags under his eyes when I saw him at the center last night."

"You were at the rec center?" Frank said. "I didn't see you."

"Maybe you guys should look past the hoop court and the weight room," Phil said. "Some of us have been trying to set up a little computer center, building a couple of Dumpster PCs."

Frank frowned. "I don't know that brand."

"It's not a brand name," Phil said with a laugh. "These are computers pieced together from components that have been thrown out. It's amazing what people will toss when they get a new system—mother boards, disk drives, cases—"

"Excuse me for butting into your little technotalk, guys," Chet burst out. "But you may remember that I was about to reveal my theory on what's going on."

"Sorry, Chet," Frank said. "Reveal away."

"Todd Coates shoved Frank down the hill," Chet announced confidently. "And the reason is simple. He wants to sabotage his uncle. What does Uncle Marv want most in the world? For the Bayport Bombers to win today. That way he can supply us with the new scoreboard, and that could help him get elected mayor. Take Frank out of the game and the Bombers don't win. They're underdogs as it is. And don't forget, Todd goes to Ocean City. He's a Slickers fan, so he'd like to see the Bombers bomb, too."

Frank's brain rushed into high gear as he thought over Chet's theory. It made sense. Maybe the glitter he'd seen after being pushed had been light reflecting off Todd's wire-rimmed glasses. He turned to Phil. "When exactly was Todd asking about us?"

"Last night."

"Where?"

"At the rec center."

"He was there last night?" Frank asked. "What time?"

"Around eight-thirty or nine," Phil answered. "He'd heard of our computer project, and brought over a hard drive from a computer he was scrapping. He got an upgrade—"

"Never mind that," Frank interrupted. "What was he wearing?"

Phil shrugged. "Jeans, I guess. What he always wears."

"And does he always wear a hooded sweatshirt?" Frank asked.

Phil thought for a second. "Sorry, Frank. I just wasn't paying much attention to any fashion statement Todd might have been making."

"What about his shoes. Was he wearing boots?" Frank persisted.

Phil's eyes lit up. "Yes, he was! Those dippy old work boots he always slops around in."

Just then Coach Moran poked his head inside the door. "Team meeting in the locker room in two minutes, Chet. Let everyone know." He gave Frank a concerned look. "You all right?"

"Everything's fine, Coach."

"I thought I saw you limping a little."

"Just a kink. I worked it out," Frank lied.

Coach Moran nodded and smiled. "Good. You ready?"

"As ready as I'll ever be, Coach." Frank stood up, ignoring the sharp stab of pain from his ankle.

Joe led the team onto the basketball court for the pregame warmup. After sinking a ball, he turned to Frank and said, "Check out who's sitting behind our bench."

Frank looked over to see Todd Coates staring back at him. Jamal sat a few rows over . . . right next to Glen Revelle.

"I'll be right back," Joe said suddenly, striding toward their bench.

"Don't start anything," Frank warned.

Joe grinned back at his brother. "I just left my sweatband in my locker. Chill out."

Joe jogged back to the locker room and retrieved his wristbands. He was just about to head back to the gym when he heard arguing in the hallway outside the locker room. Joe stopped and listened.

"I've warned you before!" an angry voice rang out. "Someone could have been killed!"

7 Kicked Out

Joe almost leaped to the locker-room door. Could the mystery voice be talking about Frank? It sounded adult—and vaguely familiar. Maybe some criminals had gotten involved in the case.

Scarcely breathing, Joe eased the door open to take a peek.

Then he sighed. No wonder he recognized that voice! It was the school principal, and he was chewing out Mr. Hooley.

"I said I was sorry I left the bucket out, Mr. Chambers," the janitor said, looking unhappily down at his scuffed, stained work boots.

"But to leave it by the *stairs!* What if someone had popped out of the locker room? They'd have tripped over that bucket and fallen down the stairs!

66

Being sorry isn't enough, Hooley. I've tried to be understanding because of your, uh, situation."

"That's just it, Mr. Chambers," Hooley said quickly. "There ain't time to get all my work done with these games and all. Y'know I'm really supposed to be back by sundown."

"That's another reason why I didn't want to go along with this little experiment," Mr. Chambers fumed. "I don't have anything against you personally, Hooley. But even your friends in high places won't save you if you foul up just once more. Understand?"

"Sure, Mr. Chambers." Hooley got busy wringing out his mop in the offending bucket as the principal stormed off.

Joe stuck his head out the door. "Cheer up, Mr. Hooley," he said. "I can't tell you how many times old Chambers has yelled at me. He's just letting off steam. After all, it's not as though you left the pail there on purpose."

"You got it, kid." Mr. Hooley grinned widely, revealing a gold tooth. "Good luck out there," the janitor said, leaning on his mop.

"Thanks," Joe replied, stepping back into the locker room.

"You're going to need it," Joe heard as the door swung shut.

Joe hit the push bar and quickly stuck his head out again. "What did you say?"

"I said you're going to need some luck out there

67

against the Slickers. They haven't lost a game since that Berman kid came off the injured list." The janitor was already mopping his way down the hall.

With a shrug, Joe headed off to the game.

The Bombers didn't need any luck for the first half of the game. Joe stole several passes, and Frank was shooting with precision. The rest of the team was tight, running through their strategies like clockwork. All of the Bombers grew more and more psyched as the points added up.

"This is almost too easy," Joe told Frank a few minutes before half-time. "We've racked up a solid ten-point lead."

Frank shook out his sweat-damp hair. "I don't know how solid it is," he warned. "If the Slickers can't crack our defense, they may begin cracking heads."

Joe remembered his brother's prediction as the Slickers played rougher and rougher. Jake Berman was a master at sneaking in the dirty plays so that the refs couldn't see. Joe got elbowed in the ribs and even had his foot stepped on. Sneaky moves, Joe thought as he dribbled the ball down the court, with Berman at his heels. Does he do the same stuff off the court? he wondered.

After yet another flagrant foul from one of the other Slickers, Coach Moran called time out and stormed onto the court. "They're playing dirty!"

the coach yelled at the referee. "Is this a basketball game or a wrestling match?"

The ref shrugged. "What can I do, Coach? I'm calling fouls and even threw out one of their guys for rough play. I don't know why you're complaining. Your team has a big lead."

"My team will be lucky to survive to the second half at this rate," Coach Moran complained as he walked back to the Bomber bench.

Joe joined the rest of the team as the coach called them around. "Don't let those guys provoke you," Moran declared. "Especially you, Joe."

"I'll keep a low profile," Joe promised. "Besides, this is Biff's game." He clapped a hand on Biff Hooper's shoulder, and with good reason. His friend Biff, playing center, had been in top form throughout the game. "You just keep it up, big guy," Joe said.

Biff grinned back at Joe. "Must be this power drink I whipped up." He offered Joe a sip from his special bottle. Biff's latest concoction was the same color as antifreeze. The one time Joe had let Biff talk him into taking a swig of this stuff, he'd wound up with a slime of blue-green algae on his teeth. Joe decided he'd pass this time.

"You don't know what you're missing," Biff said, taking a huge gulp.

"I think I do," Joe declared, eyeing the thick glop sloshing around.

The ref blew the whistle to resume play, and the two teams filed out. From center court, Berman called out to Joe. "What's the matter—you wimps can't take a little rough play? What's your coach crying about?"

"Rough play's one thing," Joe shot back. "Dirty play's something else."

"Maybe you Bombers should join the girl's conference," Berman replied.

"I guess you haven't noticed the score, Berman," Joe said with a laugh.

Berman's face went red. "First half's just a warmup."

"I hope so for your sake, Jake, because if you get any colder you'll freeze."

The Bombers passed the ball in and the game resumed. With six seconds remaining in the first half, one of the Bombers bounced a pass to Jake. Berman pivoted left, then right, trying to throw Joe off. But Joe stuck to him like glue.

Snarling, Jake shoved the ball at Joe, smacking him in the face.

Stunned by the blow, Joe angrily swatted at the ball. But he missed it, slapping Berman in the face instead.

The ref whistled Berman for a technical. Then the ref pointed to Joe and blew his whistle again. "You're out of the game, number thirty-two!"

"What?" Joe screamed in disbelief, running up

to the ref. "You've got to be kidding! What about Berman?"

Biff moved between Joe and the ref as the crowd booed its lungs out.

"C'mon, ref," Frank protested. "Berman hit Joe in the face. If you're going to throw my brother out, you ought to toss Berman, too."

"The ball that hit Joe was an accident," the ref explained. "But Joe's slap in Berman's face was intentional."

"That was an accident, too!" Joe griped.

"It didn't look accidental to me," the ref said in a stern voice. "But even so, you drew blood, and the rules say I have to toss you out."

Jake grinned as he dabbed at a tiny scratch on his cheek.

Joe couldn't believe what was happening. He had been kicked out of the biggest game of his life. His shoulders slumped as he trudged off the court and headed for the locker room. Thrown out of the game, he couldn't even stay on the bench to root for his team.

He had let his temper get the better of him. And now it might cost his team the game. A major bummer.

With Joe out of the game, Frank got the tough job of guarding Jake Berman. The coach called a time out in the third quarter. Sweating and exhausted, the team collapsed on the bench and began gulping down water. Frank felt totally drained from covering Berman, and his ankle was pounding with pain.

Frank leaned over to Biff, who was sucking in deep breaths and gulping down his power drink. "It's up to you and me, big guy," he said. "If we can just hold on to the lead—"

"Aaaaaghh!" Biff suddenly cried out. He clutched at his stomach, his face white as death. The plastic bottle he held slipped fron his fingers, spilling the power drink on the gym floor. Lurching off the bench, Biff managed to stagger a couple of feet, his body crouched over.

"Biff!" Frank yelled, jumping up to help.

But before he could reach his friend, Biff folded in a spasm of pain. His legs went out from under him.

Biff crashed to the floor with a sickening thud!

8 Poisoned!

Frank watched in horror as Biff struggled to rise to his feet. Halfway up, Biff jerked in agony and fell to the hardwood court again.

Dashing to his friend's aid, Frank didn't even notice the pain in his ankle. "Stay down," he cautioned the muscular boy. Frank dropped to his knees and eased Biff back to the floor as Chet Morton and Coach Moran hustled toward them.

"What happened?" Coach Moran asked.

"I don't know," Frank said. "He just keeled over."

Biff groaned. "My stomach . . . hurts so much . . ." He twisted in pain again.

Coach Moran looked shocked. "Chet, take him to the hospital. And hurry!"

73

Chet nodded and helped Biff to his feet. The crowd buzzed with curiosity, then groaned in disbelief when they saw the big center stagger off the court, leaning against Chet.

What a time for this to happen, Frank thought. Biff had never played a better game! Frank scooped up Biff's water bottle and sniffed it suspiciously. It had a bitter, acrid smell. He stuck the bottle inside his gym bag.

Coach Moran tapped Drew Becker, a gangly sophomore, to go in for Biff. Becker gulped nervously, then stripped off his warmup suit and joined his team on the floor. The ref's whistle blew and the game resumed.

Frank dunked three balls and intercepted two passes. He felt that his team was on a roll and that victory was a definite possibility. But near the end of the third quarter, Frank's worst nightmare came true. Berman got hot.

Really hot.

Everything he threw went in. Frank and the Bombers could do nothing to stop him. And with every shot Berman made, Frank's ankle hurt a little more.

With seconds left in the game, Frank glanced up at the clock and could see that the Bombers were still clinging to a one-point lead. But the Ocean City Slickers had the ball. If the Bombers didn't stop them now, they'd lose the game.

Berman took the inbound pass, weaving his way

74

through the Bombers defense as if it weren't there. Frank dashed over to block Berman's path. He braced himself, ready to deflect Berman's shot. But Berman spun around Frank, and before he could react, the Slicker's captain was airborne. Frank tried to jump up with him, to block his shot, but his ankle wouldn't cooperate.

Berman dunked the ball as the buzzer sounded the end of the game.

The crowd stood in stunned silence.

Berman's teammates ran over to him and gave him high-fives, whooping it up, leaping into the air and one another's arms, shouting their defiance to the hometown Bayport fans, who had begun to file quietly out of the gymnasium.

Frank sat on the floor, exhausted, dazed, unable to believe what had happened.

They had been so close.

Joe was still fuming as he and Frank walked through the parking lot after the game. "We should have had the championship all wrapped up by now," Joe complained. "I can't believe I let Berman get me thrown out—hey!" Joe stopped in his tracks. "Isn't that Todd Coates over by our van?"

Frank followed his brother's gaze. "It sure looks like him."

"I wonder what he's up to," Joe said, picking up his speed.

When Todd spotted the Hardys, he whirled from

the van and began to run away. Frank saw something twinkle as it fell from the boy and under the vehicle. Then Frank gave chase. Sprinting across the lot, he suddenly felt a sharp, stabbing pain in his ankle. He cried out in pain and stopped abruptly. Joe slowed down to see if Frank was okay.

Frank sighed and limped back to the van.

"How's the ankle?" Joe asked.

"It needs to rest, that's all," Frank said.

"Hey, Todd, wait up!" Joe yelled. But Todd Coates was already out of sight.

"It looked as though Todd was fooling around with this door," Joe said when he reached the van. The brothers examined the outside of the dark blue van. Nothing seemed out of place.

"We can always talk to Todd later," Frank said. "Let's get to the hospital to see how Biff is doing." He patted his gym bag. "And I want to get his power drink analyzed."

Ten minutes later the Hardys dropped off Biff's water bottle at the Bayport General Hospital lab to be analyzed. At the front desk, they asked for Biff's room number, then hurried to his bedside. They found him sitting up but connected to a tangle of tubes.

"You okay, Biff?" Frank asked.

"I think so. They had to pump my stomach," Biff answered in a weak voice. "I'm a little dehydrated right now, but I guess I'll survive. So, who won the game?"

"Good news first. You were voted MVP. of the game," Joe said.

"The bad news is that we lost," Frank added.

Biff groaned. "Berman finally busted loose?"

Joe nodded.

"I feel like I let the team down," Biff rasped in a barely audible voice. "I don't know what happened out there. One moment I was feeling fine. The next—"

"The next moment you were poisoned," Joe said.

"Huh?"

"We think someone spiked your drink," Frank explained.

Biff gaped at the Hardys in disbelief.

"We'll know for sure after the lab finishes its analysis," Joe said.

"Poisoned?" Biff shook his head in disbelief. "Why would someone poison *me?*"

"The why is simple. Someone didn't want us to win that game," Frank said. "The real question is who."

"A lot of people didn't want us to win that game," Biff said. "Like the entire population of Ocean City. But this is carrying team spirit a little too far."

"You don't know the half of it," Joe said. He told Biff about Frank getting pushed down the hill and the threats they'd received.

"So you feel the person who pushed Frank is the same one who made the phone call telling you to lose the game, and the same one who threw that basketball into your kitchen?" Biff asked.

Frank nodded. "We found some boot prints behind the rec center. I think they belong to the person who pushed me. The same prints were outside our house after the slam dunk through our window."

"I can't believe someone's taking this championship so seriously," Biff said. "Someone we play against is actually trying to kill us."

"Not kill us," Joe corrected him. "He just wants to make us lose."

"Don't worry," Frank said. "We'll find out who's behind this. And the Bombers can still win the championship."

"But we just lost our last game—by a lousy point." Biff gave the Hardys a puzzled look.

"We're tied in the standings," Frank explained. "And the tiebreaker is the point difference between our teams. Whoever scored the most total points in the two games we played together is the conference champ."

A wide grin crept across Biff's face. "Now I get it. Ocean City beat us by only one point today. And we beat them by only one point last time, so we're still dead even." He looked at Frank and Joe. "So now what happens?"

"According to the conference officials at the game, this is the first time it's ever happened," Frank said. "The High School Athletic Association had to make a quick decision this afternoon. There'll be another game tomorrow. We have one more chance for the championship."

Biff mustered up enough strength to give the Hardys each a feeble but heartfelt high-five.

"So hurry up and get better," Joe said. "We're going to need you."

"You know something?" Biff mumbled. "I'm starting to feel better already." Then he shook his head sadly. "But I still can't believe someone would poison me over a game. Have you got any idea who it might have been?"

"Glen Revelle was sitting right behind our bench for the whole game," Joe reminded Frank. "But why would a Rockets player care at this point if we win or lose?"

"Beats me," Frank said. "Todd Coates was sitting there, too. I talked to Jamal after the game. He'd been sitting near the two of them. But he went out to the refreshment stand at half-time for a chili cheese dog and bumped into a guy he knew at school."

"So he was gone the entire half-time," Joe said. "And that's when Revelle could have done it."

"*Anyone* could have done it at half-time," Frank told his brother.

"So where does that leave us?" Joe asked.

"Right back at square one," Frank said, pondering the situation. "Biff? Did you see anyone messing around with your water bottle? Biff?"

But Biff had drifted off to sleep.

The brothers tiptoed out of the hospital room, then stopped by the lab to get the results of the analysis. A few minutes later, they were driving out of the hospital parking lot.

"So we know that someone definitely poisoned Biff," Frank said. "The lab said there was enough rat poison to make him sick, but not to do any permanent damage."

Joe breathed a sigh of relief. "At least now we know Biff will be fine by tomorrow. We need him if we hope to win."

Frank frowned. "That's what worries me," he said. "Whoever is sabotaging the Bombers may know that, too, and try something else—"

A piercing sound interrupted Frank's words. Frank saw a Bayport police cruiser in the rearview mirror. It was blasting its siren right behind their van.

"Pull over, Frank," Joe said. "It looks like they're in a hurry."

Frank pulled over to let the other vehicle go by, assuming the police car was on the way to a crime scene. But the cruiser didn't rush past them. Sirens wailing and lights strobing, the patrol car cut them off.

"What now?" Joe said. "I didn't think we were speeding."

Seconds later a police officer jumped out of the

cruiser. With one hand on his gun, he approached the Hardys.

"Mind if I take a look in the back of the van?" the officer growled, his face grim as he looked in the driver's-side window.

"What's up?" Frank asked.

"An anonymous tip," the officer said.

"About what?" Joe asked.

The officer scowled. "Let me take a look in the back of your van, and I'll tell you. Or do you have something to hide?"

"Do you have a warrant?" Joe challenged.

"No," the officer said. "But I can get one—after I take you in for questioning. There might be a bit of a wait, and our holding cells aren't what you'd call homey."

"That won't be necessary," Frank said. "We don't have anything to hide, sir. But something tells me you're going to find something back there anyway."

"One way to find out."

"Be our guest," Joe said.

The officer opened the back of the van and shone a flashlight around. A few moments later, he said to his partner, "Found it, just the way our informant said."

Frank turned in his seat to see an open envelope spotlighted in the beam of the officer's flashlight. Several stiff cardboard rectangles spilled out of the

81

envelope. They were about the size of a baseball card but appeared to be blank. But Frank noticed there was a strip of videotape attached to one side.

"What are those?" Joe asked.

"As if you don't know," the police officer said in a scornful voice. "They appear to be phony ATM cards. And they're the reason why you two are under arrest."

9 Framed

Joe Hardy usually felt pretty comfortable in Chief Collig's office. After all, he and Frank had visited it often enough on past cases. But this time was different.

The chief sat behind his large mahogany desk and stared thoughtfully back at Joe and his brother. On a shelf hanging nearby, Joe noticed a faded black-and-white photograph of the chief and his Bayport Bombers basketball teammates from years ago.

"Chief, you know we had nothing to do with those phony ATM cards," Joe said.

"Did you know our father is the chief investigator in that case?" Frank asked.

The chief let out a loud sigh of frustration.

"Fenton filled me in," he admitted. "But when we get tips, we're supposed to follow up on them."

He waved a hand. "I know you boys have nothing to do with that ATM scam. But we did find those phony cards in your van. That's something that worries me—and your father, too. There's a large gang involved in this case. Some of the people we've arrested are hardened criminals, violent ones. But there are other bad guys still on the loose, and I'll bet they're just as vicious. Until I find out to what extent you two are involved—"

"We don't know to what extent we're involved either, Chief," Frank confessed. "Or why."

"Honestly, Chief," Joe added. "We weren't even helping Dad with his case."

Joe felt Chief Collig's eyes flick from him to his brother. "I know you two boys mean well," the chief said. "But one of these days this amateur detective stuff will get you in serious trouble. I don't want that to be on my beat or my conscience. Am I getting through to you guys?"

Joe nodded. "Is that the end of this evening's lecture?"

The chief sighed. "It may as well be. I'm just wasting my time."

"Then we're free to go?" Frank asked.

"You're free to go," Chief Collig grunted.

At the door, Joe turned and said, "Chief Collig? I have just one question."

"What?" Chief Collig asked, frowning.

"Are we still pals?" Joe asked with an innocent smile.

"Get out of here!" Chief Collig bellowed, but an unwilling smile tugged at his lips.

The Hardys hurried back outside and climbed into the van. "Well, I know who's at the top of *my* 'Let's Talk' list," Joe said as he cranked over the engine. "Todd Coates was hanging around the van earlier this evening. Maybe he saw someone planting the ATM cards."

"Or maybe that's why he was hanging around the van—to plant them himself," Frank suggested. "And I just remembered something. I thought I saw something made of metal fall from his hand when he took off. If we went back to the parking lot, I'll bet we'd find a piece of wire coat hanger with a hook in it. Low-tech, maybe, but with a little bit of practice, anyone can use it to unlock a car door—"

"Whoa!" Joe exclaimed. "Even if Todd could fiddle the door lock, where would he get a bunch of phony ATM cards? And more important, why would he plant them?"

"Try this on for size," Frank said. "Acting on a tip, the police pull over a van and find phony ATM cards. They arrest the two kids driving the van. It doesn't matter that the two are members of the Bayport Bombers. The law doesn't care very much about basketball championships."

"Okay," Joe granted. "I can see how getting us in trouble might keep us out of the playoff game. Todd could have done that to make the Bombers lose and spoil his uncle Marv's big plan. But the ATM cards—they're part of Dad's case and have nothing to do with us."

"The cards *were* in our van," Frank countered.

Joe sighed as he pulled into the driveway of the Hardy house. When the boys entered the living room, Fenton set aside the newspaper he had been reading and rose from his easy chair to greet them.

"I just had a long conversation with Chief Collig," he said. "Sounds as if you two have had a hectic day. I wouldn't worry about the ATM cards. The police know you didn't have anything to do with the scam."

The boys followed Fenton into the kitchen. Joe noticed that the broken window had been replaced. But what really held his attention was the platter of sandwiches on the kitchen counter.

"Gertrude is out tonight," Fenton explained. "She didn't know when you'd get home, so she left us these for dinner."

"Great," Joe said. "I'm starving."

"Sorry I couldn't make it to the game. I spent the day running down leads that went nowhere." Fenton pulled sodas out of the refrigerator as the boys helped themselves to sandwiches and sat down.

Their father's expression turned somber. "I heard about the Bombers' loss to Ocean City, and what happened to Biff."

Frank scowled. "We dropped off Biff's water

86

bottle at the hospital lab to be analyzed, and they found traces of rat poison in his power drink. It wasn't enough to be fatal, but it certainly gave him a rough time."

Fenton shook his head ruefully. "Some people will do anything to win. Whatever happened to old-fashioned fair play and good sportsmanship?"

"I don't know, Dad," Frank said. "But you wouldn't have found either of them in the Bayport gymnasium this afternoon."

"Do you have any idea who might be behind all this?" Fenton asked.

"We've got lots of ideas," Joe said. "Suspects-R-Us."

"At first, we thought Jake Berman, the Slickers' captain, was behind the sabotage," Frank said, a bit more seriously. "He had motive, opportunity, and means."

"But he wasn't wearing boots when we checked him out after Frank got pushed last night. And I don't think the basketball through the window is his style. Old Jake is definitely a hands-on kind of bully," Joe added, recalling how Jake had pushed him down the bleacher stairs. "Plus, I think we'd have noticed if he came across the court to poison Biff's water bottle."

"According to Jamal and Phil, Jake has a lot of thug-type friends," Frank pointed out. "They could be trying to trash our chances with or without his knowledge."

87

"Then we come to Glen Revelle, the Rockets' captain," Joe shook his head. "A lot of this is gut feeling—the way he acted when he lost, and when his father got on his case." He frowned. "Glen was sitting behind us at the game, in range of Biff's bottle."

"Glen was sitting with Jamal Hawkins, although Jamal wasn't there at half-time, when the drink was probably spiked." Frank looked unhappy. "I feel kind of awkward about suspecting Revelle. He's friends with Jamal."

"You know you can't let friendship interfere in an investigation," Fenton cautioned. "You need to be objective. If Revelle wasn't Jamal's friend, would he be your prime suspect?"

"Yes," Joe said.

"No," Frank said at the same time. They glanced at each other and laughed.

"There's one angle we haven't looked at yet," Joe added. "What if all the stuff that's happening to us is really part of *your* case, Dad?"

"How do you mean?" Fenton asked.

"Well, suppose the crooks you helped bust in the ATM scam are trying to get back at you, through us. So they went after Frank and threw the basketball through the window," Joe suggested.

"If someone wanted to intimidate me, I can think of a lot of better ways of doing it than planting some bogus ATM cards in the back of my sons' van," Fenton said.

"And if it is the same person who planted the ATM cards and pushed me down the hill, why poison Biff?" Frank asked. "How does he fit in?"

"Maybe the person thought the water bottle belonged to one of us," Joe reasoned.

"But why plant the ATM cards?" Fenton asked. "If it was the crooks, they must realize that their frame wouldn't work. Obviously, no one's going to believe you two are involved in something like this."

"Maybe they thought we'd be arrested at least, and you'd be embarrassed," Joe offered.

"It's possible, but not likely," Fenton said. "You could just as easily suggest several different people were behind each of these incidents."

"Come on, Dad," Joe said. "This case is confusing enough as it is."

With an understanding smile on his face, Fenton turned to Frank. "Do you have any other suspects in mind?"

"We did see Todd hanging around our van after the game," Frank said.

"Todd Coates?" Fenton asked.

Frank and Joe nodded.

"That's some coincidence!" Fenton exclaimed. "I spoke to Con Riley today and found out who made that 911 call after Frank was pushed."

Fenton frowned. "According to the 911 tapes, the caller identified himself as Todd Coates."

10 Suspicious Behavior

"Coincidence, my aching ankle!" Frank burst out. "I think Todd set us up with those phony ATM cards. The cops got a tip over the phone to look in the van. Now we've got Todd on the phone to 911 after the attack on me. This is definitely not a coincidence."

He frowned. "There's another connection. Phil saw Todd at the rec center last night. And he said young Mr. Coates was wearing his boots, as usual."

"So?" Joe said. "If he called 911, we know he had to be around. That would explain the prints."

"The prints up on the hill were tracked back and forth, several times," Frank went on. "That's not the trail of someone who just came on the scene.

Those are the marks of pacing by someone who was *waiting* for me."

"If Todd pushed you, why did he call 911?" Joe asked.

"Maybe to divert suspicion from himself. Todd's a smart guy. He knows we're detectives," Frank said. "There's one more point—the gleam I saw before I passed out. It could have come from Todd's wire-rimmed glasses."

"You make a strong case," Fenton admitted. "But why would Todd try to hurt you?"

Joe explained Todd's stormy relationship with his uncle. "Maybe he felt it was the only way he could get back at his uncle. Maybe he hoped to ruin Marvin Coates's chances of getting elected by wrecking our shot at winning."

They sat in thoughtful silence for a few minutes, turning their attention to Aunt Gertrude's sandwiches. Frank finished his, then said to Joe, "You said before you'd like to talk to Todd Coates. Well, we've got more reasons to now." He glanced at his watch. "Phil said Todd works part-time for his uncle. It's just early evening. He might be at the office now."

"So what are we waiting for?" Joe said, halfway out of his chair.

The boys waved goodbye to their father and headed outside. Soon Frank was pulling the van into an open space on Bayside Drive. One side of the street was lined with buildings. The other was a boardwalk that ran along the bayfront. As they climbed out of the van, Frank saw a sleek Jaguar turning the corner.

"Isn't that Marvin Coates's car?" Joe asked.

"Could be," Frank said. "Well, if the uncle was working late, maybe the nephew still is."

Frank took a deep breath of salty ocean air and gazed out over the sparkling twilit waters. In the sky above the gulls were making a racket as a fishing trawler returned to port.

The brothers strolled along the boardwalk opposite the Bayside Warehouse, a long, gray, weather-beaten building. A sign above the wide delivery doors identified it as Marvin Coates Enterprises.

"Not exactly what you'd expect for a rich businessman's headquarters," Frank observed. "It looks a little shabby."

"Don't forget this whole area's going to be developed," Joe said.

"*Was* going to be developed, remember? The project's on hold," Frank reminded his brother.

The Hardys crossed the street, walking up to a small door next to the delivery entrance. Frank rang the bell set in the door frame, and they were promptly buzzed in.

When they reached the top of the stairs, a door opened and a pretty young woman poked her head out. She seemed surprised to see the Hardys. "Can I help you?" she asked in a perky voice.

"We're here to see Todd Coates," Frank said.

"I don't think he's here."

"Was that his uncle Marvin's sports car we saw leaving?" Frank asked curiously.

The woman pushed a strand of blond hair off her forehead. "Yes, it was. I'm Kim, his secretary. He was on his way to the Bayport rec center to work out." She gave the boys a dubious look. "Was Todd expecting you?"

"Yes, ma'am." Frank gave the secretary his most innocent smile. "If you'd just point us toward Todd's office . . ."

The woman paused a moment, then said, "I guess that would be all right. It's on the lower level. Go back down the way you came and go down another flight."

"Thank you, ma'am," Frank said.

The Hardys made their way down two flights of stairs and a hall to find Todd Coates's office. Frank knocked, but there was no answer. He opened the door and flicked on the lights.

It was a small windowless space. Most of the room was taken up by a large worktable thrown together from two short filing cabinets and several wide boards. An impressive-looking, state-of-the-art computer sat in the middle of the table. Loose diskettes covered almost every square inch of desktop.

A poster of a rock group was pinned to a door against the far wall. Joe strode across the room and opened the door. Beyond was a large, empty utility closet.

"Uncle Marv didn't exactly give his nephew the penthouse suite, did he?"

"Find him?"

The Hardys spun around to see the secretary standing in the doorway with a set of keys in her hand.

"I guess we must have just missed him," Frank said.

The secretary smiled. "Better luck next time. Todd has his own key and comes in at odd hours." She followed the boys out of the warehouse. At the door, she locked up after them, then headed for her car.

As the Hardys crossed the street to reach their van, Joe suddenly turned toward the boardwalk. "Hey, Mr. Hooley, how's it going?" he called to a man approaching them.

Frank glanced over to see the school janitor looking extremely surprised, his jaw slack as he looked back and forth at the brothers.

Recalling the conversation he had overheard between the janitor and the school principal, Joe added, "I thought you weren't allowed out after dark."

Joe grinned, but a worried expression flashed across the older man's face. Then he gave them a crooked smile. "Finished late at the school, but I wanted to stop by here." Mr. Hooley nodded toward the building that held Coates's office. "I spoke with Mr. Coates the other day about a custodial position, just in case Mr. Chambers let me go. He's a fine gentleman, that Mr. Coates, and he told me to call him up if I ever needed any help."

"He's not in the office now," Frank told the janitor. "His secretary said he went over to the rec center for a workout."

"Just my luck." Mr. Hooley sighed. "Oh, well, maybe I'll catch him tomorrow."

"You'll probably be working late again, Mr. H.," Joe said. "Tomorrow is the big game."

"So it is." Hooley gave the boys a smile, showing off his gold tooth. "Good luck again."

The smile quickly faded as he headed back up the boardwalk, his body hunching into the stiff onshore wind.

"Hey, Mr. Hooley! Could we give you a lift?"

"Uh, no thanks," the janitor called over his shoulder. His words seemed almost torn away by the wind.

"What was that all about?" Frank asked.

"I heard Mr. Chambers chewing him out just before the game," Joe replied. "They made a big thing out of Mr. Hooley's 'special situation.' Apparently, he's got a strict curfew. That's what I was kidding him about." Joe shook his head. "I'd say Mr. Hooley is too old to be living with his mom. Maybe he's got a very strict wife."

"I don't think that would impress a school principal," Frank objected. "From the looks of things, Mr. Hooley's curfew would have to be more official."

"What are you getting at, brainiac?" Joe said.

"I think our Mr. Hooley may be living in a halfway house," Frank replied.

Joe stared at him. "Come on, Frank," he said. "Mr. Hooley—an ex-con?"

"Not quite an ex-con," Frank said. "People in halfway houses are still serving prison terms, even if they're allowed out to work during the day."

Not entirely convinced, Joe shrugged and said, "Well, at least now we know why he was talking with Marvin Coates. He must have told Hooley to give him a call about a job." He grinned as he unlocked the door and got behind the wheel of the van. "One question answered. For our next— where to now?"

Frank shrugged. "Phil Cohen told me that Todd Coates stopped by the computer room at the rec center yesterday. Maybe he's there again tonight. You want to check it out?"

"It's worth a try," Joe said.

As soon as they entered the front door of the rec center, they saw Todd coming out of the crafts room on the main floor.

"Hey, Todd. Todd Coates!" Frank shouted. "We want to talk to you."

Todd didn't answer. The second he saw the

Hardys, he took off down the hallway. Frank and Joe started after him. Todd reached the stairway at the end of the hall and darted downward.

"There's an emergency exit on the lower level," Frank said. "That must be where he's heading."

Todd had made it down one flight when the Hardys reached the stairs. Frank saw him glance back as he and Joe barreled toward him.

But something went wrong as Todd skidded around to the next flight. His feet seemed to slide out from under him on the landing.

With a wild yell, Todd tumbled helplessly down the stairwell!

11 A Slippery Situation

"Todd! Are you okay?" Joe cried out, charging down the stairs. Todd Coates was sprawled out on the basement landing. His glasses had flown off and lay beside him.

But before Joe reached Todd, the door to the men's locker room opened to reveal a tall, orange-haired young man—Glen Revelle. "What's going on out here?"

When Glen got a look at Joe and Frank, he snarled. "You two!" He quietly leaped over Todd to block their way to the boy. Glen's fists were clenched, and he looked ready to swing at Joe. "What did they do to you, buddy?" Glen asked Todd. "If you want to lodge a complaint—"

But Todd didn't hang around to talk. He scooped

up his glasses, scrambled to his feet, and dashed into the locker room. Glen still stood in their way, aching for a fight.

Joe was wondering if he'd have to go through Revelle to get to Todd when he heard a familiar voice.

"Is there some sort of problem, boys?"

Joe turned to see Marvin Coates coming down the stairs. He was wearing sweats, and a white towel was wrapped around his neck.

"Hi, Mr. Coates," Frank said. "We wanted to talk to your nephew, but he suddenly took off."

"Oh," Marvin said, toweling his face. "Well, don't mind Todd. He was probably avoiding me, not you two."

Glen Revelle looked confused for a moment. Then, with a snort of disgust, he thrust past the Hardys and Coates, heading up the stairs.

Coates watched him go. "That boy played on the Rocky River team, didn't he?"

"Yeah," Joe said. "He took their loss pretty hard."

"Speaking of which," Coates said, "it was a shame about the game this afternoon. What happened to the Hooper boy in the second half?"

"He was poisoned," Joe said bluntly.

Coates gasped. "Poisoned? Are you sure?"

Frank nodded. "The hospital lab analyzed the contents of his water bottle. It still held traces of rat poison. Not enough to kill, but more than enough to make even a big guy sick."

"But why?" Coates asked.

"Obviously, someone wanted us to lose that game," Joe said.

Coates shook his head in disbelief. "I can hardly believe it. Do you have any idea who would do that?"

"We're doing our best to figure that out," Frank said, not wanting to discuss the case with so many suspects in possible earshot.

Joe could see that Frank intended to say no more, so he quickly changed the subject. "Lucky for us we still have a chance to win the conference championship. There's going to be another tomorrow."

"Yes, I heard about that." A bead of sweat trickled down Coates's cheek, and he wiped it away. "Will the Hooper boy recover in time to play?"

"Probably," Frank said.

"Fortunately, our buddy has a cast-iron stomach," Joe commented. "It would take more than a little rat poison to sideline him."

"Good, good," Coates said. "Well, guess I'll go for a quick dip before I hit the sauna. Good luck in tomorrow's game."

"Thanks, Mr. Coates," the Hardys said together. They followed Coates into the locker room, but

Todd was no longer there. "I bet he bombed right out of here," Frank said, nodding toward the emergency exit. They quickly searched the locker area.

"Well, he's not in the showers. But he could have ducked into the pool." Joe pushed on the other door that led from the room.

The smell of chlorine hit Joe's nose as he and Frank stepped into the pool area. A quick glance around showed a couple of swimmers, but no Todd. "Either he's holding his breath in the pool, or he's hiding in the girls' locker room."

A loud splash drew the boys' attention. Joe's eyes picked up two bodies swimming underwater toward them, side by side like twin torpedoes. Then two familiar faces suddenly broke the surface of the water near the edge of the pool where they were standing. Iola Morton and Callie Shaw grinned up at them.

"Think fast," Iola said, splashing water on Joe.

"Hey!" Joe said, taking a step back.

"Why don't you guys join us for a swim?" Callie asked.

"We can't right now." Frank's eyes darted restlessly about the pool area. "Have you seen Todd Coates?"

"I don't think I'd know him if I saw him," Callie said.

"Maybe I'll check out the parking lot," Frank said. "You coming, Joe?"

"I think I'll swim a few laps before the rec center closes," Joe said. "Report back to me at nine o'clock sharp."

Frank grinned and gave his brother a little salute as he exited the pool area.

In the locker room, Joe pulled his swim trunks out of his locker. He changed, wadding up his clothes to stuff them into the cramped locker, already jammed tight with basketball trunks, sweats, unwashed T-shirts and socks, and several pairs of old sneakers.

Joe spotted Marvin Coates, off in one corner by himself, getting dressed. Marvin noticed Joe and gave him a friendly nod as he slipped on a pair of expensive-looking loafers. Joe waved back.

Grabbing a towel, Joe slipped into his rubber thongs and flip-flopped out of the locker room and back to the pool area. Leaving his flip-flops and towel on the bench near the locker-room entrance, he let out a war whoop and dove into the pool.

After Joe dunked Iola a few times in revenge for splashing him earlier, he told the girls about Biff being poisoned and about the ATM cards that had turned up in the back of their van.

"Why would someone try to frame you?" Iola asked. "It makes no sense."

Joe shrugged. "That's what we're trying to figure out. The cards looked the same as the ones the police confiscated when they busted the criminals Dad was chasing down."

"Wow," Callie said. "You've had a busy couple of days. Phone threats, attacks, windows broken, and now a brush with organized crime. I'm surprised you have time to play basketball."

"Well, it is the championship, after all," Joe said, splashing Callie playfully.

"Not only that, the whole school can't wait to see that new scoreboard you're going to win for us," Iola said.

Callie splashed Joe back, then pushed off, going to one of the lanes for swimming laps. Joe and Iola hung on to the side of the pool and continued their conversation.

"It seems that no matter where I go, everyone is talking about Marvin Coates and that new scoreboard," Joe said.

"Then you should come to my house," Iola said. "My father won't let us even mention Marvin Coates."

Joe's eyebrows rose. "Why?"

"Dad is on the town planning commission, and he's mad because Mr. Coates pulled his money out of the bayfront project."

"It didn't say that in the newspaper story," Joe said.

Iola shrugged. "Oh, Dad says that was all politics and string-pulling. But he wouldn't trust Marvin Coates to come up with the price of a hot dog, much less a scoreboard."

"Well, I can see why your dad's upset. I guess

we'll just have to keep on Mr. Coates's case—*after* we win the championship."

Laughing, Iola pushed off from the side of the pool. "Spoken like a true sportsman." When she was already a few feet ahead of Joe, she suddenly cried, "Race you!"

Joe pushed off and swam as fast as he could for the other side of the pool.

The three teenagers swam laps until ten to nine, then the girls pulled themselves out of the pool and left for the dressing room. Five minutes later Joe climbed out of the pool. The swim was just what he had needed. He felt relaxed, and his muscles tingled from the workout.

Joe strode over to the bench where he'd left his towel and thongs. He figured he'd just have time for a hot shower before Frank came back. He quickly toweled off, but where were his flip-flops? Joe searched beneath the bench, but his shoes weren't there.

"Another one of Iola's little jokes," Joe muttered with a smile. Then he spotted the missing thongs over by the edge of the pool. He crossed over to them, slipped them on, and turned to leave the pool area.

Suddenly, his feet went flying out from under him.

Crack!

Joe's head hit the concrete edge of the pool. He

could feel his body roll over, splashing into the pool, but was powerless to stop himself.

Joe's muscles weren't reacting to his brain's frantic commands as he sank like a deadweight. He could only watch the surface recede as he sank deeper and deeper under the water.

12 Lights Out

What was that? Frank wondered as he opened the door between the locker room and the pool. The sound was something between a *splosh* and a *plop*, as if someone had tossed a sack of potatoes into the water.

Frank glanced around the pool area. No one there—and no one around the lockers, either. Where had Joe gone?

Just as he was turning to leave, something in the pool caught Frank's eye—a single flip-flop floating on the water.

With a sense of dread rising up in him, Frank stepped closer to the edge of the pool and saw a human form sinking to the bottom.

Fully dressed, Frank dove into the water, knifing

downward toward the blond-haired figure. It was Joe!

Seconds later Frank was hanging on to the side of the pool, supporting his brother as Joe sputtered and coughed up water.

Frank noticed an angry-looking red welt on the side of Joe's forehead. "What happened, little brother?" Frank asked after pulling Joe up onto the pool deck. "Dive into the pool and bang your knucklehead on the bottom again?"

"Ah, c'mon," Joe said, carefully touching the sore spot. "I was eight years old when that happened." He made his way over to the pool bench and angrily grabbed his towel. "All I know is I put my thongs on, and about two seconds later the concrete's kissing my forehead."

Frank noticed the second thong near the pool ladder. He retrieved the thong and rubbed his index finger over the bottom. It felt oily.

"Your flip-flop's been greased." Frank inspected the slick substance. "Looks like Vaseline. A lot of swimmers carry it for chapped lips from being in the water so much."

Frank could see blood pumping at Joe's temples. "I want to know which guy put that stuff on my flops," Joe said angrily. He tossed Frank his towel and said, "I would have drowned if you hadn't come when you did."

Frank had been thinking the same thing, but

didn't want to say it. Drying himself off, he followed his brother into the locker room.

"Did you see anyone in the pool area besides Callie and Iola?" Frank asked, stripping off his wet clothes. Luckily, he had a reasonably clean set of sweats in his locker.

"No one," Joe admitted. "But I was swimming laps, and it's pretty hard to see much from inside the pool. It would've been easy for anybody to monkey with my thongs. They were next to the bench, and the bench is right near the locker-room door."

Frank put on his sweats while Joe changed into his street clothes. "We'd better make tracks. It's already past closing," Frank said.

"Where to?" Joe asked, slamming his locker shut.

"Home," Frank said firmly. "We should get some ice on your head. Unless you want to be sporting a goose egg at the game tomorrow."

They arrived home to find the place empty. "Aunt Gertrude's still taking care of her sick friend, and Dad's out on a case," Joe announced, reading a note in the kitchen.

"Just as well," Frank said. "Then I can throw this stuff in the dryer without answering twenty questions."

He was wringing out his jeans down in the basement laundry area when he felt something squishy in the back pocket. Digging inside, he found a soggy lump of green paper—the remains of a paper airplane.

"Oh, *man!*" Frank burst out, charging up the stairs.

He found Joe in the kitchen, munching on one of Aunt Gertrude's leftover sandwiches. "What's up?" Joe asked.

"That fall down the hill must have rattled my brains," Frank said, carefully unpeeling the soaked paper. "The night I got pushed behind the rec center, we found that program with the telephone number written on it. It's been sitting in my pocket ever since."

"So it took a swim with you," Joe commented, watching Frank's carefully working hands.

Frank sighed with relief as he unfolded the crumpled wad to reveal the telephone number. The scribbled digits were blurred, but he could still read them.

Joe glanced at the number, punched it in on the kitchen phone, then handed the receiver to Frank.

"I can't believe I forgot—" Frank stopped speaking as the phone on the other side of the connection was picked up. "Coates residence," a pleasant female voice chirped in his ear.

"Uh—ah, is Todd in?" Frank improvised.

"I'm afraid not." The voice on the other end sounded a bit less friendly. "Would you like to leave a message?"

"Um, no—no. I'll catch him later." Frank hung up and stared at the phone for a moment. Then he turned and reported his conversation to Joe.

"Todd has some serious explaining to do," Joe said angrily. "Those *must* have been his boot prints we saw. That means he wasn't just passing by when he saw you pushed down the hill—he was the one who ambushed you! The program must have fallen out of his pocket while he was waiting."

"Hold on a minute," Frank said. "Why would Todd have his own number on a program?"

Joe was stumped. "You got me on this one," he admitted to Frank. "I think my brain might be waterlogged."

It didn't make sense. Nor did it make sense for any of their other suspects to have Todd's number. Jake Berman and his bully friends weren't likely to pal around with Todd. And Glen Revelle didn't even know the guy.

Frank stared in frustration at the soggy green paper. He'd hoped it might provide some answers. Instead, it just seemed to raise new questions.

As Frank headed for the locker room the next afternoon, he felt as unhappy as Mr. Hooley looked, mopping the halls under the eagle eye of Mr. Chambers. With a deep breath, Frank tried to shove away all the unanswered questions of the last few days. He had to get suited up for the championship match.

Chet Morton shook his head as he looked over the Bombers sitting on the locker-room bench and standing by their lockers. "I dunno, Frank. Between your ankle, Joe's head, and Biff's green face, we already look like the team that lost."

"Bite your tongue!" Joe commanded.

Frank knew it would be a tough game. And someone had been doing everything possible to see that the Bombers lost. If only we'd solved the case before this final game, Frank wished. But he wasn't going to let himself feel defeated before the game even started. Instead, he'd work out his frustration on Jake Berman and the Ocean City Slickers.

The game was tight from the opening tip-off. Frank's ankle was a lot better, but Biff was still a little weak from the rat poison. At half-time, the score was tied.

Frank knew from experience that it took Berman most of the first half to warm up to his full playing intensity. And he was right. By the fourth quarter Jake was hot.

Joe tried to keep Jake covered. It took every ounce of strength he had to keep up with this top player, who was not only strong and fast, but also wily.

With only minutes left in the game, and Joe draped all over him, Berman drilled another basket. Even as he shot, Joe rammed into him. The ref whistled Joe for the foul.

"I've been hearing a bunch of stupid rumors

111

about the Slickers trying to sabotage the last game," Berman spat at Joe as he headed for the foul line. "Let me tell you something, Hardy. I don't need to cheat to beat you guys. I can do that playing blindfolded." As if to demonstrate his point, Berman shut his eyes and threw the foul shot in.

Joe took the inbound pass and dribbled up court. Berman dogged him all the way.

"It's over for you guys," Berman said, reaching in and trying to steal the ball.

Joe dribbled the ball out of Berman's reach and raced up the court. He bounced a pass to Tony Prito, racing along at his flank. Berman stayed on Joe.

"You're looking tired, Hardy," Berman mocked. "Maybe you're out of your league."

With a burst of energy that tapped all his reserves, Joe tore ahead on the race to the Bombers' basket. He took Tony's pass, dribbled once to get to the basket, double-faked his shot to get Berman in the air, then threw up a soft fade-away that eased through the hoop, hitting nothing but net.

Jake came down hard on Joe, fouling him.

"Bombers! Bombers!" The crowd's cheer resounded throughout the stands as Joe stepped up to the foul line and calmly sank the foul shot.

The Slickers' coach signaled for a time-out.

But Berman waved his own coach off. Gathering

his team about him, he screamed at them, "I am *not* going to lose this game!"

Frank could hear his bellow halfway across the court.

Still fuming, Berman took the inbound pass and dashed the length of the court. Tony tried to block the shot, but Berman stuffed the ball in Tony's face. Then Berman jumped in a twisting layup to tie the score with only ten seconds remaining in the game.

Biff passed the ball in to Tony. Frank took Tony's pass, dribbled twice toward the basket, tossed a no-look pass to Joe in the corner, and continued to the basket. Joe's pass had eyes, finding its way through a crowd of defenders as if it were a missile homing in on its target.

Frank was waiting for it. He caught the ball, spun around Berman, and, riding a tide of pure adrenaline, slammed the ball through the hoop at the exact moment when the room was plunged into darkness.

13 In the Dark

An almost indescribable storm of noise blared at Joe through the sudden pitch-blackness. He could hear the yells of terror, the rattling of the bleachers as people tried to get away, and the pounding feet on the floor of the court.

Joe also caught the sickening sound of bodies falling as people tripped in the darkness. Then came the even worse screams of pain.

It felt like a nightmare come true, and Joe had no idea how long the confusion continued. Then, at last, a calm but firm voice rang out over the tumult. "Hold it! *Hold it!* This is Police Chief Collig. Remain in your seats. There's no reason to panic. We've just got a power failure of some sort."

The noise lessened as the chief continued. This

114

time he gave orders. "Will the security guards nearest the double exit doors please open them?"

Joe heard a metallic rattle as the school security officers hit the crash bars on the emergency exit. The large double doors swung open. Though the wintry afternoon sky was fading fast into dusk, a dim light filtered into the gym.

Even Joe had to admit to feeling a little relief at the return of illumination. Now he could see the police and security guards heading toward the bleachers. Assisted by school officials, they carefully began moving the sports fans out of their seats and down to the court. Though the spectators could not see where they were going, they filed out in a more orderly way. Officers were also attempting to help those who'd been injured in the brief panic.

Chet began handing out warmup suits to Joe and his teammates. "I can't tell whose is whose in this light," Chet said. "Just put 'em on and let's get out of here."

Joining the thinning crowd outside, the Bombers stared back at the deserted gymnasium.

"What happened in there?" Biff Hooper wondered.

"More important, what does it mean to the game?" Tony Prito wanted to know.

"I made that last shot, just as the lights went

115

out," Frank said. "I heard the ball swish into the net. But I don't know if that's proof enough that we won the game."

"We definitely won," Joe said. "Only once again, something—or someone—stands in our way of the championship."

"Hmm. No lights in the school—or the parking lot," Frank observed.

"But the streetlights are on," Joe observed. "And those houses across the street are lit up," he added, pointing.

"So it's not a blackout or anything," Frank concluded.

Joe glanced at his brother. "I don't know about you, but I don't plan to just stand here letting my sweat freeze."

"Me, neither," Frank agreed. "Let's go."

"Where?"

"What do we do in our own house when the lights go out?"

Joe brightened. "Check the circuit breaker?"

"That's right," Frank said with a nod. "Where there's electricity, there's got to be a circuit breaker. So let's go find it."

Frank and Joe told their friends they'd be back and then made their way around to the side of the school. Weaving through the exiting vehicles, they picked up a flashlight from their van and headed back to the building.

"Here's the entrance to the locker rooms," Joe said, pulling open a door. Frank flicked on the flash. Following the beam of light, they cut through the locker room and made their way into the tunnel that led to the basketball court. But instead of heading to the arena, they turned toward a metal door marked Stairs at the opposite end of the passageway.

They descended the stairs until they found themselves inside a gloomy-looking basement. The air was warm and stuffy, smelling of machinery and oil, cleansers and sweat.

Frank shone the light around what appeared to be a fairly large room. The single dim beam fell on an oil-stained workbench that sat beneath several rows of bare pipes. Next to the bench stood a cart full of cleaning supplies.

"This must be Janitor Central," Joe joked.

Frank pointed the beam of light around, revealing all sorts of tools and repair equipment. Joe began to circle the room, surveying stuff tossed into oily old cardboard boxes stacked on metal shelves, or just dumped here and there on the floor.

He was so busy looking around, his foot accidentally smacked into a new shoebox holding a few dozen metal wing nuts.

Frank's light flicked toward the box as it flipped over, showing clean white print: Acme Work Boots. The metal bolts inside scattered all over the bare concrete. They sounded as if someone had just dropped about a hundred dollars' worth of pennies.

"So much for quiet snooping," Frank said.

Even in the darkness, Joe could feel his face turning red. "We need more light, Frank," he complained. "Where's that circuit breaker?"

"Let's check in there," Frank said, shining the light on a door that stood half open.

They entered the room. Frank played the flashlight beam along the wall as the two boys squinted into the darkness.

"There it is," Frank said, shining the light on a gray metal box whose front panel stood open.

The boys crossed the chilly room and peered inside. They found dozens of small labeled switches and one large master switch. The master switch had been shut off, then smashed with something large and heavy. The smaller switches had also been battered.

When Joe reached out to the wrecked circuit breakers, Frank grabbed his wrist. "Those controls might be broken up enough to give you a nasty shock if you put your finger in the wrong place," Frank warned.

"Well, I think we've seen enough, anyway," Joe replied. "Let's get back upstairs and tell the chief—"

Joe heard a sound behind them and spun around. Frank's flashlight was pointed in the opposite direction, but some light bounced off the wall. It was enough to reveal a dim figure, a figure leaping toward them.

The shadowy shape slashed down at them with a length of battered two-by-four!

14 A New Suspect?

Frank had half a second to dodge the length of heavy wood sweeping down at him. It just wasn't enough time to get completely out of the way. The club smashed onto his flashlight, tearing it from his hand.

The Hardys' only source of light fell to the floor, rolling away.

Frank hopped back, the fingers on his right hand numb from the shock of impact. Metal banged against his shoulders, telling him he'd backed up against the wall where the circuit breaker box hung. There was nowhere else to go.

His attacker was barely a silhouette in the darkness. Frank raised his arms, but that would be no protection against another swing.

Then Joe's shadow came hurtling into the fight. "Frank! Duck!" Joe's voice rang out.

The mystery attacker reeled as Joe rammed into him. The club came down to crash against the metal box, but Frank had ducked under it.

He leaped up, grabbing the length of wood before the guy could swing again. But the attacker would not let go of his weapon.

They lurched around the room, Joe wrapped around the man's middle, Frank wrestling for the club. Then Joe stumbled on the flashlight.

All three of them went over, crashing to the floor. The good news was that the attacker lost his wooden weapon. The bad news was that Joe's grip on the guy was also shaken.

The mystery man wriggled loose like an eel, then took off through the room. Joe was already dashing after him.

Frank scrambled and got the flashlight. "I want just one good look at this guy," he muttered.

The chase had moved into the larger room. The banging and crashing sounded as though Joe and the assailant were tripping over every box in the place.

Frank lunged into the room, aiming his flashlight. The beam caught Joe's shoulder, the other man's foot . . .

But when Frank aimed for the guy's face, all he lit was the large plastic garbage bag the man was hefting. The bag burst, and the air filled with scraps of paper. Frank barely got a glimpse—a yellow gleam. Then the guy disappeared in the blizzard of paper.

"Come on!" Frank yelled. The Hardys stormed up the stairs, reached the passageway—and were nearly blinded as a pair of heavy-duty police flashlights were shone in their faces.

"All right, you two, hold it!" one officer yelled. Frank's dazzled eyes could see that the man in blue had his hand on his gun butt. "What were you doing down there?"

"We were chasing the guy who trashed the circuit breaker downstairs," replied a furious Joe. "Did you get him?"

"We just got here from the gymnasium," the other officer said.

Frank glanced down the passageway. "Then he must have ducked into the locker room."

Even from that distance, they could hear the slam of the side door.

The police officers lowered their flashlights. "You say this person smashed the circuit breaker? Can you give us a description?"

Frank suddenly realized the man was staring intensely at him. And now that Frank could see more than a uniform behind a blazing light, he knew why. This was the officer who had searched their van and found the phony ATM cards.

"Hello again, Officer." Frank sighed. "Maybe we should go and have a chat with the chief."

Back home, as Frank and Joe were finishing a late supper with Aunt Gertrude, they heard their father's car in the driveway. Minutes later Fenton joined them at the dinner table.

Gertrude passed Fenton a plate, but he shook his head. "I had dinner with Chief Collig," he explained. "He gave me quite an earful about the power outage at the gymnasium."

"An 'outage' makes it sound like the electric company's equipment failed," Joe complained. "Some nut pulled the master switch in the circuit breaker, cut the lights, then bashed everything up so it couldn't be fixed."

"Sabotage again," Fenton said. He looked thoughtful for a long moment.

Frank nodded. "The worst yet. People in the bleachers got hurt in the first panicky rush. And nobody knew how long it would take to get the lights back on."

Joe explained that Frank had sunk the ball just as the lights went out, but that no one actually saw it happen.

"Well, then, I have a later news bulletin," Fenton said. "The circuit breaker will be repaired overnight. There will be school tomorrow."

Joe rolled his eyes. "That ought to make a lot of kids happy."

"And the school and athletic association officials have met," Fenton went on. "There's to be a replay of the entire game tomorrow night."

"So we still have a chance," Frank said with a sigh of relief.

"My heart's too weak to take too many more of these close games," Aunt Gertrude protested, her eyes twinkling.

"This has been about the craziest basketball season I've ever had," Frank admitted.

"Not to mention the other sports we took part in today," Joe added. "Baseball, with that guy trying to use your head for batting practice."

"I'd say football, from the way you tackled him," Frank said with a grin.

"I was going to suggest wrestling," Joe kidded back. "If we keep this up, we'll be ready for the pentathlon."

Frank's smile faded. "When you come down to it, what we were really playing was tag. Too bad we didn't get a look at who was playing 'It.'" He looked over at Joe. "You were right on top of the guy. Didn't you notice anything that stands out in your memory?"

With a shrug, Joe offered, "He smelled pretty bad."

Frank rolled his eyes. "You could probably say that about half the guys in school."

Thinking a bit more seriously, Joe said, "He had a beeper on his belt. I noticed it when I had my arms wrapped around his waist. But a lot of guys in school would have them, too."

Frank barely heard the rest of what his brother was saying. Joe's first words had sparked a memory—a memory of someone who normally *wouldn't* have a beeper.

"Mr. Hooley," Frank blurted out.

"What?" Joe echoed in disbelief.

"Who?" Fenton and Aunt Gertrude both asked.

"Mr. Hooley is the janitor at our school," Joe explained.

Frank picked up the conversation. "He also has a beeper on his belt. I heard it go off once. At the time, I thought it was sort of funny—you know, the high-tech custodian. Now, though . . ."

"Ah, come on," Joe protested. "This is Mr. Hooley we're talking about. The guy who pushes a mop around."

"The guy who has to be *somewhere* before nightfall, remember? Who refused a lift to get there?" Frank turned to Fenton. "I think he's staying in one of those halfway houses that let prisoners out to work during the day."

Fenton's eyebrows rose. "Maybe I could check that out," he said. "Do you have a first name for this Hooley?"

Frank shrugged helplessly. "Mister."

"You're hanging this guy just because he wears a beeper!" Joe complained.

"What about this last bit of sabotage?" Frank

asked. "Whoever wrecked that electrical panel must have had knowledge of the setup under the gym."

"*We* found that panel," Joe countered. "And we'd never been down there before in our lives."

"The rat poison that knocked Biff out of the game!" Frank said triumphantly. "That had to come from somewhere. I bet you'd find some in those shelves of supplies in that Janitor Central place."

Joe didn't have a quick answer to that.

"And remember that box you knocked over?" Frank went on. "It was brand-new and said Acme Work Boots."

"Objection," Joe stated, seeing where Frank was going. "I've seen Mr. H.'s boots—they're all stained and crummy-looking."

"Sure, the tops would look that way after he slopped disinfectant all over them with his mop," Frank said. "But I want a look at the bottoms of those boots—the soles, the treads. Maybe we could match them to some footprints we've seen."

"You've suggested some things about means and opportunity," Fenton spoke up. "But what about motive? Why would this janitor try to ruin your team's chances for the championship?"

"I heard our principal threatening to fire him." Joe started out almost reluctantly, but his voice picked up speed. "Maybe Hooley's mad at Mr.

Chambers—and Bayport High in general. He wants to get back by making us lose."

"And don't forget the new scoreboard," Frank said. "He might want to prevent us from getting that."

"Right," Joe agreed. "That, too."

"But there's one thing that doesn't fit," Frank said. "Those fake ATM cards that turned up in our van."

"He might have read about the arrests and connected your names and mine," Fenton suggested.

"And if he's a crook, maybe he could get his hands on phony cards," Joe said. "It could still be an attempt at sabotage. He probably hoped that the police would keep us at the station overnight after they found the planted cards. Then we'd be too tired to play in the game."

"You've got a circumstantial case," Fenton said. "The janitor apparently has motive, opportunity, and means. Now all you need is solid proof."

"We may have a witness," Frank said excitedly. "Todd Coates phoned in the 911 report when I was attacked. He was near our van when those ATM cards showed up."

"But he ran away as though he was afraid of us," Joe said. "And he did it again at the rec center."

"But was he afraid of us," Frank speculated, "or of whoever he saw, such as Hooley? Maybe we need somebody else to reach out to Todd—someone he'd listen to."

"Phil Cohen," Joe said promptly.

"My thought exactly." Frank rose from his seat, then stopped. "Sorry. Aunt Gertrude, you made a great meal. But could you excuse us?"

"Go on," his aunt said with a smile. "I know how you boys get with your mysteries."

Frank went to the kitchen and made a brief phone call.

"Phil's not at his house—he's at the rec center," Frank announced when he returned. "Feel like taking a ride, Joe?"

"Do I?" Joe fairly exploded from his seat.

"Meanwhile, I'll talk to some connections on the force and see what I can find out about Mr. Hooley," Fenton offered.

Frank had to fight himself to keep the van from screeching to the rec center at top speed. When they arrived, they found Phil at his improvised computer workshop.

"I think we've got this honey up and running," Phil said. He beamed down at a battered computer case with wires leading to other boxes. It looked like something from a high-tech junk shop. But Phil smiled at it with the kind of look guys usually reserved for their baby brothers or sisters.

"We've got the big hard drive that Todd Coates gave us, and also a fax modem that he dug up," Phil explained. "So now, we can talk over the phones to other computers."

"Actually, Todd's the reason we came to se[e] you," Frank said. He ran through their suspicions about Mr. Hooley, and the fact that Todd may have seen the janitor doing something he shouldn't have.

Phil's eyes were wide by the time Frank finished. "Well, sure, I'll be glad to help you out. We were going to test the modem by trying to get online with Todd at his uncle's office."

"Wait a second," Frank said. "We've got a modem at home. I bet that's how my dad is checking out Mr. Hooley. Could we call him first and see if he got anything?"

"Sure," Phil said, his fingers dancing over a dingy computer keyboard. "Is there a special phone number?"

Frank gave the number, and after a moment, Phil announced, "We're connected. Your dad is on the other side."

Leaning over the keyboard, Frank typed: "Dad, it's Frank. Anything yet on Mr. H.?"

Seconds later, the reply came. "Interesting record," Fenton typed. "Especially his associates. Sending file."

The screen blinked, then an image appeared. It was a police record, topped with a mug shot of a slightly younger-looking Mr. Hooley.

"That's our guy, all right," Joe said.

Frank was already studying the arrest record. "They got him for bank fraud," he said. His eyes

the section marked Known Associ-
names seemed to leap out at him:
tch. Henry Desmond. Cletus Skratos.

Desmond, Skratos," Frank read aloud.
they sound familiar?"

Joe did a double take as he stared at the screen.
"Frank!" he said. "Don't you remember Dad's
story about the arrests they made? Those are the
guys who got picked up for the ATM scam!"

Frank's jaw sagged. "So Hooley is connected
somehow with Dad's case? I don't believe this!"

He turned to Phil. "Can you save this to a file?"

Their friend began hitting keys, but the screen
flickered again, this time going blank.

"We crashed!" Phil said in annoyance. "I'm
afraid Todd left too many files on the hard drive. I
really should have erased them."

Phil called up the directory of the disk. Rows of
file names appeared on the screen. But before Phil
could type the command to delete them, Frank's
hand landed on his wrist.

"Can you get into these files?" Frank demanded.

"Well, yeah," Phil said. "There's a program on
the disk—"

Frank was already tapping a finger on the screen,
pointing to a file that said Byzantin.

A couple of keystrokes later, and the screen filled
with figures. "Joe! Look at this!" Frank cried.

Joe stared with a puzzled frown over Phil's

shoulder. "Looks like a bunch of financial records to me."

"But look at the name of the company," Frank said, tapping the screen. "The file name jogged my memory."

"Byzantine Importers! That's the phony company Dad said was a cover for the ATM scam."

Frank nodded. "Looks as if we have *two* connections with Dad's case. These are all Todd's files."

Joe looked at his brother in disbelief. "You mean . . . *Todd Coates* is the criminal mastermind Dad's trying to put away?"

15 The Genius and the Janitor

Joe Hardy turned from the screen, with its incredible information, to Phil Cohen. "You said Todd Coates is waiting for a modem call from you at his uncle's office?"

Phil nodded, wordless.

"That's all we need to know. Come on, Frank!"

The Hardys jumped into their van, and Joe drove to the Marvin Coates Enterprises' bayfront warehouse. The lights were out—in fact, the place seemed deserted.

"You think Todd's here?" Frank asked doubtfully, looking at the dark building.

"We can't tell from the outside. That basement office doesn't have any windows." Joe climbed into the back of the van and reappeared with a crowbar and a flashlight.

"What are those for?" Frank asked.

"In case Todd doesn't answer the door," Joe replied.

They'd just gotten out of the van when Joe spied a figure hurrying along the boardwalk. As the approaching man stepped into a pool of light from one of the street lamps, Joe ducked down. "Here comes Mr. Hooley," he said in a low voice.

"He's out past his bedtime," Frank whispered as the janitor rang at the front entrance. Hooley was quickly buzzed in, heaving the metal door wide as he entered.

Counting on the loud rasping buzz to hide any noise he'd make, Joe bolted for the door. He managed to hook the heavy slab with his crowbar just before it swung closed. Bracing the door open, he beckoned to Frank. "B-and-E," Joe whispered, handing the flash to his brother. "Buzzing and Entering."

They gave Hooley a moment or two to get downstairs, then crept into the warehouse. Frank flicked on the flashlight and shone it around. Nothing. They descended to the lower level, wincing at every creak of the old wooden steps.

The hallway to Todd's office was deserted, but a crack of light showed beneath the door. Joe put his ear to the door and listened.

"You hear anything?" Frank whispered.

"Zip," Joe replied softly. He slowly turned the handle, pushed the door open a few feet, and poked his head in. "Empty."

The Hardys stepped inside the office, and Frank headed straight for Todd's computer, switching it on.

"You looking for something in particular?" Joe asked.

"Anything," Frank said, browsing through several directories. He brought up a list of businesses, tapped some more keys. "Considering what we found on the disk drive he threw out, who knows what we'll find here." He leaned forward. "Check it out. These are accounts showing where the money from Byzantine Importers went!"

Joe set the crowbar down on Todd's desk to peer at the numbers on the screen.

"So, you finally got here." Todd's voice came from behind them. "That's breaking and entering, man."

Picking up the crowbar, Joe whipped around and put Todd in a headlock, hauling him through the doorway. "With what you have on that computer, I don't think you'll want to call the cops," Joe said. He let Todd go, and Todd didn't try to run off or fight.

"Phil Cohen told us you were a computer whiz," Frank said. "Creating computer viruses is one thing. But programming phony ATMs for a jillion-dollar scam—that's not too smart."

Even with Joe still holding the crowbar in his fist, Todd's expression was cool as he stood there. Calmly, he stated, "I didn't scam anyone."

"Yeah, right," Joe scoffed. "Just like you didn't plant those ATM cards in our van."

"Actually, I think he's telling the truth," Frank said, looking just as surprised as Joe was.

"What?" Joe burst out. "But the evidence is right there in his computer."

Frank shook his head. "The mastermind's gang has been operating for more than ten years. Todd hasn't been running scams from the cradle. And these files? They were downloaded from another computer—user ID Kim."

"That's my uncle's secretary," Todd volunteered.

"Now you're trying to tell us that your uncle's *secretary* is the kingpin?" Joe asked with an incredulous laugh.

"Joe," Frank said, turning from the computer. "It's not the secretary, it's—"

"I suppose Killer Kim is the one who attacked Frank outside the rec center," Joe cracked.

"No, I'll take credit for that," came a new voice from the door.

The Hardys and Todd spun around. Hooley was leaning against the door frame. He smiled, and the light reflected off his gold tooth.

"You know," Frank said from the computer desk, "when I looked up the hill after my fall, I saw something glinting up there. Who'd have thought it was your gold tooth?"

"So I fooled you," Hooley said with a satisfied smile.

"You left enough clues, we just didn't put them together," Frank said. "The boot prints . . . Marvin Coates's phone number on that program." Frank had quickly figured out that the number was to reach Todd's uncle, not Todd, though the boy lived at the same address.

"I was wondering where I lost that," Hooley admitted. "Mr. Coates gave me his number—"

"But you lost it," Frank said. "That's why you had to go to his office."

"You must have poisoned Biff at half-time," Joe said. "The rat poison was probably in one of those bottles on your cart. Who'd have noticed you cleaning up around our bench?"

"That's right, sonny boy," Hooley replied. "I'm also the one who called you and told you to lose the game. And I wrote the threatening note on the ball that smashed through your kitchen window. The ball came from the team's equipment room. Easy enough to steal, since I have the key."

"How did you know I was swimming at the rec center the other night?" Joe asked.

"I can answer that one," Frank said. "The same way he knew to hit the circuit breaker right before the end of the game: He's got a beeper."

Hooley smiled and patted his belt, where the beeper was attached.

Frank frowned. "Marvin Coates was at the center that night. We just never put it together."

Joe began to get angry as he saw what Frank was getting at. "Yeah, old Marv was around when I nearly got drowned." He glared at Hooley. "Did he grease my sandals himself, or did he call you in? And what about those ATM cards you planted on us? What was that about?"

Hooley stared. "I don't know what you're talking about, kid."

"But the ATM scam is what started all this," Frank said. "Marvin Coates Enterprises is just a front for money laundering. No wonder Marvin could throw the bucks around. He had a literal money machine to back him up. But when Dad busted the operation, Marvin Coates's cash stopped flowing. That's why he pulled out of the bayfront development program."

"And he couldn't afford a big expensive scoreboard," Joe added, leaning back against Todd's desk.

"I got the job of fixing that. It should have been easy, sabotaging a high school basketball game," Mr. Hooley growled. "But you two junior detectives kept getting in the way. The boss just sent me down to get his nephew. I wonder what he'll say when he sees—"

While Hooley was talking, Joe let his hand rest on a wooden storage box for computer disks. With a twist of his wrist, Joe hurled the diskettes in Hooley's face.

As Hooley ducked, Frank made his move. He snatched up the crowbar Joe had set down and slapped it against the side of Mr. Hooley's head. The janitor was out cold before he hit the floor.

"Come on!" Todd cried. "We've got to get out of here!"

He leaped through the doorway. But a second later, he reappeared, walking backward with his hands in the air.

Marvin Coates followed his nephew, a Colt Python pistol in his hand. "Drop whatever you used to nail Hooley," he commanded.

"He's got us," Joe said loudly, shooting Frank a look as he noisily dropped the empty wooden box to the floor. From the corner of his eye, he saw Frank tuck the crowbar behind his back as Marvin Coates came in.

The crime boss scowled down at the groaning Hooley in disgust. "A bungler. I should never have taken him on again. Unfortunately, my regular crew was behind bars. Thanks to Fenton Hardy." He glared threateningly at Frank and Joe.

At that moment the secretary poked her head inside the door.

"Bring the car around, Kimmy," Coates told her

curtly, lowering the gun. She nodded and darted away.

Coates sneered at Todd. "My little nephew, the computer whiz. Getting all the dirt on Uncle Marv, huh?" he said, glancing at the computer screen. "I should have destroyed those files long ago. Well, better late than never." A few keystrokes, and the screen was clear—everything deleted.

"Too bad you couldn't erase your promise to buy our scoreboard just as easily," Frank said in a calm voice.

Coates gave him a wry smile. "Almost immediately after I held that press conference, one of my cop sources told me your father had grabbed my money-making machines. There I was, high and dry. The money I'd so foolishly pledged to my old school is now all the cash I have left in the world."

"But you only had to part with it if the Bombers won the championship, right?" Joe asked hotly.

"Exactly," Coates said. "It wouldn't help my chances of running for mayor if people saw me breaking a promise. And Hooley owed me a favor for getting him that janitor's job."

"You were his friend in high places," Joe said.

"I helped him get in the work-release program." Coates scowled. "All he had to do was sabotage a high school basketball game." Coates looked disgusted as he said, "Child's play, and he couldn't pull it off. Well, I'm finished with him now."

He looked at the boys. "And now it is time to wrap up Marvin Coates Enterprises. There's a lovely young lady waiting for me in a car outside. And there's a bag with what's left of my ill-gotten gains in the trunk. But, to help us make our getaway—" Coates gestured with the gun. "Carry Hooley into that closet."

Frank, Joe, and Todd did as they were told. The Hardys each took a shoulder, Todd picked up the unconscious janitor's legs, and they carried out their grim task. Todd turned to leave the closet first, but before he could step out, Coates banged the door shut.

In the blackness of the enclosed space, Joe scrambled over Hooley's inert body and slammed his shoulder into the door, desperately putting all his weight behind it. But too late.

Coates slid the deadbolt in place.

Standing in the darkness, Joe could very clearly hear the sounds of liquid being slopped around. Then he smelled gasoline.

"Sorry, boys," Coates said from outside the door. "But I can't have any witnesses."

16 The Getaway

Joe was furiously rattling the locked closet door as Marvin Coates left the office.

"We're going to need the crowbar, Frank," Joe said in the darkness.

With crowbar in hand, Frank groped to the door, searching for a spot where he could begin wedging their way to freedom. "Too bad Coates didn't come a step closer," he grunted, setting to work. "I wouldn't have minded using this on his head."

"Less talk and more work," Joe said urgently. "I think I smell smoke!"

"So do I," Todd said in a shaky voice.

With all his strength, Frank pushed against the crowbar. Wood splintered as the door opened a

141

crack, and Joe's fear proved to be true. Smoke seeped into the closet.

"Give me a hand!" Frank yelled, coughing. He and Joe heaved together. The door opened a little more, but the lock still held them in.

Frank reared back, launching a frantic karate kick where he figured the bolt should be. With a noise like a scream, the lock tore off and the door flew open. The office was uncomfortably warm and full of smoke, but there were no flames—yet.

"The fire is still upstairs. We've got to get out of here—now!" Frank gasped.

Pulling their shirts up over their mouths and noses, the Hardys reached down, both grabbing an arm of the still semiconscious Mr. Hooley. They dragged the janitor out into the hallway with Todd Coates following.

In the corridor, the smoke was much thicker. Black smoke attacked their eyes. Frank blinked back tears.

"Where's the staircase? I can barely see!" Joe hollered, going into a violent coughing jag.

"This way!" Todd yelled.

Frank pulled Joe and Todd down to the floor, where there was more oxygen. Following Todd's lead, the Hardys lugged their unconscious burden along. The smoke was even worse when they reached the base of the stairs. Todd began to cough uncontrollably and suddenly fell to his knees.

"Joe, help Todd!" Frank shouted.

"Can you handle Hooley alone?"

Frank coughed. "No problem. I carry big potbellied guys up burning stairs all the time."

Joe helped Todd to his feet. "See you outside."

Grunting, Frank lifted the limp form of the janitor over his shoulders in a fireman's carry. He's heavier than he looks, Frank thought. Each step upward became a struggle against Hooley's weight and the smoke that made Frank sick and dizzy. Halfway up, his foot crashed through a burning plank.

Frank slipped. The janitor's weight pinned him down. Frank lay there dazed, gasping for oxygen, slipping off into darkness. . . .

Then strong hands grabbed him under the arms, and he felt himself being hoisted up over someone's shoulders.

Opening his eyes a few minutes later, Frank found himself stretched out on the boardwalk across the road. Joe stared down at him with a worried expression. "You all right?"

Frank nodded and sat up. "What—?"

"I got just a bit concerned when you weren't behind me, so I popped back to look for you."

"And Hooley?" Frank asked, greedily sucking in the fresh, salty sea air.

Joe nodded toward a wheezing form lying beside Frank. "Todd's in the van talking to 911 on our phone. The fire department's on the way, and Todd is telling Chief Collig about the leased helicopter his uncle keeps parked on his estate. It seems Kim, the secretary, is also a pilot."

"Well, what are we sitting here for?" Frank rose, and the night spun giddily around him. "You drive," he said.

As Frank pulled himself together on the ride to the Coates estate, Todd Coates watched him with worried eyes over a soot-streaked face. "You guys go through this all the time?"

Frank grinned. "Hey, this is a piece of cake. Of course, you helped to mix things up a bit. Oh, umm . . . sorry. I guess I forgot to thank you for calling 911 when I got pushed at the rec center. But why did you plant those fake ATM cards in our van?"

"I was intending to talk to you that night," Todd said. "But when Glen Revelle went at you guys, well, I got scared off."

He took a deep breath. "I suspected that my uncle was involved in organized crime for a while. One day, I was snooping around, and I found those cards by Kim's shredder. I didn't know what they were till I saw something on the news about ATM fraud, and about how your father helped break up the scam."

"You had the evidence. Why not go to the police?" Frank asked.

Todd shrugged. "Everyone knows that Uncle Marv and I don't get along. And since that nonsense with the computer virus, who was going to take my word over my rich, famous uncle's? But, according to Phil Cohen, you guys had a solid rep as detectives."

"So you went to talk to me, but you got scared off," Frank said.

"I'm not the world's bravest guy." Todd stared at the floor of the van. "But I figured if I got you involved, if the cops found the ATM cards in your van, you'd have to solve the case. I didn't know you were already involved, thanks to my uncle and that Hooley guy. I just got you into trouble when you were already in danger. Sorry, guys. Really."

"Don't worry about it," Joe said. "If we were put off by little stuff like that, we wouldn't be detectives."

"*Little* stuff?" Todd echoed. After that, he only spoke to direct them to the Coates estate.

Joe steered the van up a winding road until Marvin Coates's mansion came into view. The house stood on the edge of a wind-swept cliff overlooking Barmet Bay and the Atlantic Ocean beyond. But a wrought-iron fence stood in the Hardys' way.

"There's a keypad that opens the lock," Todd began.

"No time for that!" Joe yelled. He brought the van up till the bumpers met iron, then gunned the engine. Metal groaned. Then suddenly the van exploded through the gate in a spray of sparks that tore the front bumper off.

"Could I ask you guys a question?" Todd said in a tight voice. "Do you . . . like . . . ever have trouble getting car insurance?"

"Let's put it this way," Joe said, laughing. "We've learned a lot about body work."

"Where's the helicopter landing pad?" Frank asked.

"Around back, near the cliff." Even as Todd spoke, they heard the roar of a helicopter engine coming to life.

Following the sound, Joe stomped on the accelerator, aiming the van at a large hedge. The van bulldozed its way through, its headlights illuminating a small concrete square on the ground with a bull's-eye painted on it.

Looking like a huge dragonfly, the helicopter was about to take off.

Joe zoomed straight for it.

"I don't believe this," Todd cried. "We're playing chicken with a chopper!"

17 One Good Shot . . .

Joe gritted his teeth as the van barreled forward. But the helicopter was lifting off right in front of them. And straight ahead was the cliff's edge, only twenty feet away.

Hitting the gas, Joe steered the van through a wild skid that brought them almost to the brink of the long drop to the water below. Safely stopped, he brought up his hand, his thumb and index finger about an inch apart. "Missed it by this much."

"The helicopter or the cliffside?" Frank asked sarcastically. He gazed over the edge of the cliff, across the turbulent blue-green sea, trying to spot which way Coates's helicopter had gone. "I guess we just wait for Chief Collig—"

The steady *thwump-thwump-thwump* of an approaching helicopter cut off his words.

"It's the police chopper!" Joe shouted.

The copter's cargo-bay door burst open and Con Riley waved them over. The boys quickly boarded the bird, and it lifted off the ground, turning even as it rose into the air.

The swifter police chopper soon had Coates's escape craft in sight. Seconds later, they were flying above it. Joe wondered if Coates and his secretary had even spotted them.

"Now what?" Frank said.

"We can't shoot them down," Todd said.

"I have an idea," Joe spoke up. He pulled several lengths of chain, maybe eight feet long, from a canvas bag lashed to the side of the fuselage. "I saw this in a movie once. They used some cable, but this should do the trick."

"What are those things?" Frank asked.

"They're used to tie down aircraft in rough weather," Todd explained.

Joe counted out the lengths of chain. "We have six of them. If we can entangle one of the chopper's rotor heads, these babies will wrap around the pitch rods."

A wide grin creased Frank's face. "In other words, Kimmy won't be able to steer."

A wicked smile curved Todd's lips. "That's right. She'll have to bring it down."

148

"I'll go up front and tell Con and the pilot what we're up to," Frank said. "Let's wait until we're above the ocean. I don't want Coates crashing through the roof of someone's house."

A moment later Frank returned. "When we're above the water, the pilot will take this chopper down as close as he can. Joe, I'll hold on to you while you play bombardier and toss the chains."

"Gee, thanks," Joe said as he slid the cargo-bay door open. A blast of wind and noise hit them. Joe took several chains in his hands. Frank got securely braced inside the bird, then took a good grip on Joe's belt. Seconds later they were above the ocean. The police chopper swooped to within feet of the fleeing helicopter, so close Joe could feel the police chopper shudder in the slipstream of Coates's helicopter. Joe felt he could almost reach out and grab the fleeing craft's rotors.

He let go of the first chain. It missed the blade by inches, rattling off the side of Coates's chopper. Then he dropped the second one. A complete miss. He dropped the third one. Kim managed to swerve the helicopter away at the last second. He dropped the fourth one.

Bull's-eye.

Coates's helicopter suddenly plummeted downward toward the sea, zigging and zagging crazily as Kim tried to maintain control.

It hit the water with a big white splash.

Todd stared down at the sea in frozen horror. "For their sake I hope the coast guard arrives soon. That water's freezing."

"Bombers! Bombers!"

Joe didn't know what was louder: the chanting of the crowd, the stomping feet, or the beating of his own heart. He took a deep breath to calm himself.

Bayport's coach had just called his last time-out. They had time for only one final play—a give-and-go. Coach Moran looked Joe in the eye. "Joe, I know you love to shoot, but I want to see you pass this time!"

The ref blew his whistle for play to resume, and the Bombers and the Slickers trudged back out onto the court. The crowd came to its feet for the final seconds of play.

"Bombers! Bombers!"

Joe broke free of his man and took the inbound pass. Immediately, two Slickers came running for him. Great, Joe thought, now I'm double-teamed. Dribbling through heavy traffic, Joe was relieved when Frank appeared, setting up a pick to block Joe's guards so he could get free again. Adrenaline pumping through his veins, Joe leaped up like a gazelle, soaring high into the air.

In a fraction of a second, his eyes took it all in, as if the game had suddenly shifted to slow motion. Jake Berman had sniffed out the play—he'd intercept the pass if Joe tried it.

In midair, Joe shifted the ball from his right hand to his left to avoid the block, twisted his body sideways, and dunked the ball inches from Berman's face.

The crowd erupted—standing, cheering, screaming, and howling with delight—as the buzzer sounded, ending the game.

The bleachers quickly emptied of Bayport fans, who spilled out onto the basketball court. They mobbed Joe, patting him on the back, slapping high-fives, finally lifting him onto their collective shoulders and carrying him around the sports arena.

"We're number one! We're number one!" they chanted.

Frank, also riding high on the shoulders of his teammates, ended up next to Joe. He shook his head in amazement. "Great shot, Joe. This is one time I'm glad you *didn't* follow orders."

Joe gave his brother two thumbs-up as they were carried into the locker room for a post-game celebration. "I just hope Coach feels the same way!" Joe shouted back.

Todd Strasser's
AGAINST THE ODDS™

Shark Bite
The sailboat is sinking, and Ian just saw the
biggest shark of his life.

Grizzly Attack
They're trapped in the Alaskan wilderness
with no way out.

Buzzard's Feast
Danger in the desert!

Gator Prey
They know the gators are coming for
them...it's only a matter of time.

Published by Simon & Schuster   2023-01

BILL WALLACE

Award-winning author Bill Wallace brings you fun-filled
animal stories full of humor and exciting adventures.

Published by Simon & Schuster   648-33/01

**The Fascinating Story of
One of the World's Most
Celebrated Naturalists**

Celebrating
40 years
with the
wild
chimpanzees

MY LIFE *with the*
CHIMPANZEES

by JANE GOODALL

From the time she was girl, Jane Goodall dreamed
of a life spent working with animals. Finally, when she
was twenty-six years old, she ventured into the forests
of Africa to observe chimpanzees in the wild. On her
expeditions she braved the dangers of the jungle
and survived encounters with leopards and lions
in the African bush. And she got to know an amazing
group of wild chimpanzees—intelligent animals whose
lives bear a surprising resemblance to our own.

Illustrated with photographs

A Byron Preiss Visual Publications, Inc. Book

Published by Simon & Schuster

2403-0